THE BOOK OF
TORMOD

A TEMPLAR'S APPRENTICE

KAT BLACK

SCHOLASTIC PRESS
NEW YORK

For my brother
Billy

Book design by Christopher Stengel
Map by Kayley LeFaiver

Library of Congress Cataloging-in-Publication Data

Black, Kat.
  A Templar's apprentice / by Kat Black.
    p. cm. — (The book of Tormod)
Summary: While trying to harness his power for prophetic visions, a fourteenth-century Scottish boy joins a Templar knight on his sacred quest to unearth an ancient relic.
        ISBN-13: 978-0-545-05654-0 • ISBN-10: 0-545-05654-3
1. Templars — History — Juvenile fiction. [1. Templars — Fiction. 2. Knights and knighthood — Fiction. 3. Clairvoyance — Fiction. 4. Apprentices — Fiction. 5. Adventure and adventurers — Fiction.] I. Title.
  PZ7.B52896Te 2009
  [Fic]—dc22   2008014212

10 9 8 7 6 5 4 3 2 1   09 10 11 12
                    Printed in the U.S.A.   23
                    First edition, February 2009

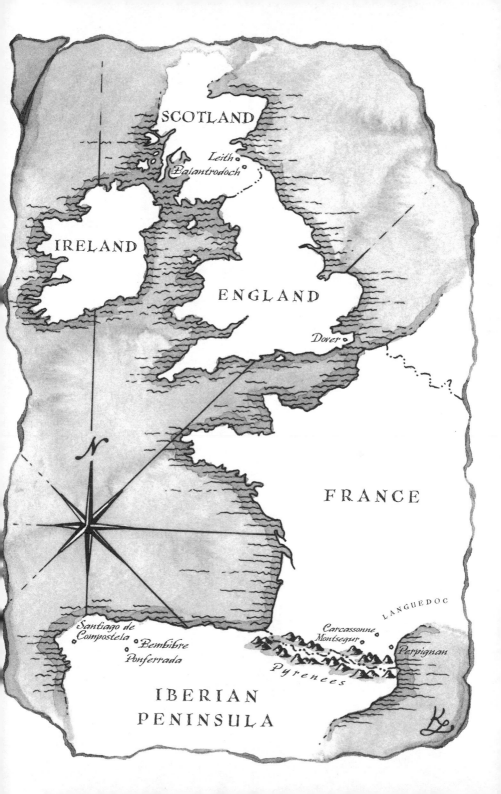

PART ONE

AN UNFORESEEN DUTY

It was the first of May in the year of Our Lord 1307. . . .

✠

The sun was sinking deep in the late spring sky. Its red and orange hues streaked the heavens with a strange and eerie light that made the dark of the woods shadowed and frightening. A creep of green moss covered the trunks of the trees, and old wet leaves covered the paths. It was not a night I wanted to be walking alone, but I had no choice in it.

Dung-heap cheater! The words pounded in my head. *I cannot believe that I took ye at yer word.* The breath of the forest whispered along my neck. The night air was changing, growing cold as the sun sank, but I was hot, inside and out.

Go get it, Tormod, he had said. *Can ye no' see that I'm busy, ye gomerel?*

My stomach twisted at the memory of my brother's tone and words. *Busy, aye! Busy making eyes at Bridie MacDonald,* I thought.

My hands were fisted tight and my face was hot. No doubt the freckles on my nose and cheeks were standing out, just as they had when Torquil ordered me to go for the box of tinder. Just as they had when Bridie had laughed and said, "Will ye just look a' him. His face is as red as his hair."

My hair was red. Not the soft auburn red of the burn as it washed over the rocks on its way to the sea, but more the ruddy orange of a freshly cut carrot.

I ran my fingers through the offending mess. Sweat from my jog had made the hairs stick out like the spikes of an urchin — a result of my mam's latest shearing. The lice had infested the household and she'd chopped the lot of us.

I was one of nine. Not the oldest or the youngest, not even the middle, I was thirteen, and seventh — the seventh son. The one who was never still, never quiet, never listening. I was different.

Someday I'll get out o' here, I thought angrily, and not for the first time. *They'll miss me an' be sorry!*

The wail of a bagpipe floated toward me from behind and I broke into a run. My breath quickened. *The festival.* Da would be furious if the lighting of the Beltane fire did not go off on time. And he'd not blame my brother Torquil. It would be me that felt the strap. My backside ached at the mere thought of it.

He'd not listen if I told him that Torquil had traded duties with me. He'd not care that I had done *all* of Torquil's hauling and stacking of the wood for the bonfire. No. All he would see was that I had delayed the festivities by not fulfilling my duties.

I stretched my stick limbs to make greater strides as I came in sight of the hut. As it was, I'd have to run the whole way back to the village to make it to the ceremony on time.

Our hut of stone and thatch was bigger than most of the dwellings spread across the hillsides. It had started out small but grew as the family did. I ran around the back and through the door closest to the animal stalls. The cows started and stomped at my arrival. "Be still, ye big hairy beasts. 'Tis just me, Tormod."

The hut was quiet. Our home was never truly free of people, and so the lack of sound was strange to me. The rest of the family was back in the village. Tonight was the celebration of Beltane, the beginning of true summer, a time for giving thanks. My brothers and sisters and I had joined with the families of the neighboring crofts to prepare. We had cleaned the square, even scrubbed down the enormous boulder in the middle, and cleared the old rushes from the kirk. The smell of the hay that had covered the dirt floors still filled my mouth and clung to my plaid.

The rush cart was filled with new straw and fresh flowers, and the celebration was ready to begin. It would start with the procession of the cart, led by Jordy MacFie, the village piper. Jordy had been waiting when I ran off.

The skirl of pipes sounded and my heart dropped. There was to be a feast, with storytelling and music, and a tremendous bonfire would burn straight through 'til morning. Well, that is if I ever made it back in time.

I, Tormod MacLeod, was to bring the box of tinder that would give spark to the great heap of wood I had helped stack for most of the day. Bringing the material that would start the fire was an honor, but not one I had planned on.

"Where is it?" I shouted. The box of tinder should have been on the shelf next to Mam's weaving. "Why is naught where 'tis supposed to be? Too many bairns," I grumbled. "Too many hands touching, and moving, and playing with things."

I was fair flying through the rooms of the hut like a squall, tossing aside everything in my path. I snatched up the twins' coverlet and the small tin box I was looking for bounced on their pallet. *What a relief.*

I was nearly to the door when the crunch of gravel beneath the heavy tread of a horse stopped me dead in my tracks.

"Da," I whispered. The lump in my throat threatened to steal my breath. I edged to the window, peeled back the oilcloth shutter, and peered outside.

AN UNEXPECTED VISITOR

"Come out, lad. I can see ye standing there."

My first look at the man brought a rack of shivers through me. He wore a black hooded cloak drawn close about him. And when he lifted his arm and called me forward, I saw a flash of silver glint beneath. I hesitated, frightened. Then a strong gust of wind blew back the cloak and beneath it I saw the white of vestments, a second cloak, and an armless tunic. The edge of a bright red cross glowed in the dim light.

I had never spoken to a Knight Templar before. My cousin Angus was in training as one of the Holy Brethren, but I didn't think he counted as yet. I moved quickly to the door and bolted outside, crossing the space between us.

"Aye, Sir Knight?" I gazed up at his looming form. Though I was considered a fair size for my age, I was still small next to him. My head didn't even come to his knees as he sat the enormous black horse of war.

"Where's yer father, lad?" His voice was soft and lilting, his brogue even more pronounced than mine. My mother was of the Highlands and my father of here in the Lowlands. We were a mix of dialect in my home.

"Gone to the village with the rest," I said.

"Everyone?" he asked. His fingers tightened on the horse's reins, making the animal balk.

"Why do ye need them? Is there something I can do?" I was eager to offer something of worth to the knight. I stared at him hard, taking in every detail of his presence. Even seated as he was, I could see that he was big. His shoulders were wide and his legs were long. His eyes were deep and dark, a brown so very brown they were nearly black. He had a thin beard that began beneath his nose and flowed long over his chin. Hidden as it was, I could not tell the color of his hair, but his beard was brown with silver shot through.

"Do ye know the way to Balantrodoch?" he asked.

I was so caught up in my inspection it took a moment for his question to sink in. "Aye. I do. 'Tis beyond the forest, just over three leagues from here." We all knew of the preceptory. It was the grounds of the main fort of the Knights Templar in this province.

He looked into my eyes a long moment, as if reaching deep into my soul to measure my worth. "I have a duty for ye, lad, one that is o' utmost importance."

I could barely contain my excitement.

"I need ye to deliver a message to the Abbot. Can ye read?"

The question seemed out of place in what he had been asking, but I answered nonetheless. "No, sir. We had a schoolmaster for a while, but he moved on and none has come since." I cringed with embarrassment. It was not unusual to be without the ability to read. There were no more than a few in the village who could. Still, it bothered me to be seen by the Templar as something less than what I might be.

The knight seemed relieved at the reply. He pulled from his side bag a rolled parchment. The seal in the wax was the crest of two knights on a single horse. He handed it over and a strange tremor passed through me at the contact. "Tell no one. Go quickly."

I was afraid then. The box of tinder cut into the palm of one hand and the parchment dented softly in my other. *They expect me a' the bonfire. Da will thrash me within an inch o' my life. Mam will worry.*

He motioned me on. "No one, lad," he repeated sternly.

A duty that is secret. Excitement rippled through me. *Someone else will run for the box of tinder. Probably Torquil.* With a grin I ran back into the hut and tossed the tin box onto the coverlet.

A DUTY REQUIRED

It was nearly dark. The wind had risen. I felt the strength of it — the last press of winter. It whipped through my tunic and breeks as I hurried. I was glad of my plaid, an enormous bolt of tartan cloth I had wrapped tight around me and pulled up over my head like a cloak.

I took the path behind our hut, up over the hills. It was rough country. The rocks were sharp. They dug into the thin soles of my boots, but I paid them no heed. I was my da's runner. I carried messages from one end of the village to the other, about the catch or the crew's arrival back on land. We were fishers. We had two boats and many nets.

The wood sat at the top of the hills. Its inky silhouette towered above me as I climbed, driving out the little bit of confidence I felt when the Templar had asked me to go. My backbone trembled. At the forest's edge I hesitated, but with little choice but to get on with it, I took a deep breath and plunged from bare light to none at all.

Inside the ring of trees, the wind stopped as if it had been snuffed out like the flame of a candle. I would have been glad of it, but the cold that remained was worse. The dark lay heavily on me like a shroud. The spot behind my knees trembled.

Cautiously I moved, focusing on the feel of my feet as they landed. Rocks and twigs, dirt and jutting roots clutched at my mind and soles. I paid great heed. The path through the wood was short, but I had never done the trek by night. It was unnerving. My heart leapt and started every few paces, and thoughts of the evil tales Torquil told of this place haunted me.

At nearly the half point, something rustled behind me. I turned and stared hard in the direction I had come. I could see nothing, but I *felt* it. Life stalked in that darkness.

My breath was loud in my ears. I tried to quiet it, to listen for what was there, moving fast to put distance between it and me. Suddenly my foot came down on a bit of unsteadiness. My body pitched forward with no way to stop, and the scroll fell free.

Sticks and rocks bit into me as I cast around, frantic. I had to find it.

A hazy danger lurked at the edges of my thoughts. Dry leaves crackled. I groped about wildly, searching until at last my fingers closed on the soft edge of the scroll.

Eyes tracked my movements. It was nearing. The tension in its limbs was coiled.

Starting up into a crouch, I peered through the endless darkness, fingers now seeking something I could use to defend myself.

But what I encountered in the last sweep was not what I had expected. Atop a cold mound of leaves, I felt the edge of another parchment.

Two scrolls! Two? I thought in shock. My breath rushed out in a burst.

A rustle sounded closer on my left.

My heart was near moving my ribs in its haste to beat. I rummaged through the leaves ready to bolt if I could do nothing else. Just then, my fingers closed over a palm-sized rock with sharp edges. I hefted it, as a small, glowing set of amber eyes met mine.

It was a boar, a female, a new mother. I was near her litter.

Go easy, Mother. I stared, willing her to feel that I was of no harm. Moments trickled by as we faced off. Then with a soft grunt, she turned and waddled away.

I was lucky. If she had chosen to charge, I might not have been able to outrace her. Though her tusks were not long, they were a danger.

I rose, legs trembling, now thinking on the two parchments tucked reverently against my chest. What might have happened had I not, by chance, come upon both? I was nearly faint to think on it.

My sense of direction was twisted. I let my mind drift, feeling the life of the wood flow through me. *Water behind. Mountain ahead.* I blinked then shivered. *Ahead.*

With great care I made my way through what was left of the forest. It seemed a lifetime before I came on a break in the trees, where faint light brightened the gloom. I stopped, finally able to breathe and examine the damage.

I brushed away most of the earth that clung to the outside of the sealed scroll. It seemed fine, just barely dented. The loose parchment was a bit worse. A smudge of dirt nearly obscured the first line, and the edge was crimped where my hand had closed on it.

I could not read, as I'd told the Templar, but looked on it nonetheless. Rough edges of land and waving lines of water were inked there, along with hills and a sketch that resembled trees. Placed over it all was a series of dots I guessed must be towns.

Off to the side a box was drawn, a close-up of a place from the land. Inside the box was a waterfall flowing down from a mountain surrounded by a forest. Lower, down in the corner was a small, strange silhouette. It was hard to make out in the dark, but I got the impression that it was a figure, shown from the back, with arms stretched up to the skies.

The map itself was old, the parchment thin and the edges crumbling. As I stared, a brisk wind set upon me and nearly lifted the fragile document from my fingers.

Carefully I rerolled the page and slid it back where it belonged. From the outside it looked no different. Praying the Abbot would be none the wiser, I took off at a jog. I'd lost time in the woods. I had to hurry.

The run was not the longest I'd ever done, but by far my fastest. The terrain flew by, as did the candle marks. I came on the preceptory during the night.

Balantrodoch was the largest and most important preceptory encampment of the Knights Templar in Scotia. I had seen it once. Torquil had hiked with me when I had begged him to come, but that was before he decided to hate me. It was painful to think on it. Torquil abandoned me, chose his friends, and left me with nothing but the dream of getting away.

I moved to the edge of the last rise. A long swath of dark stretched before me. *Balantrodoch.* It sat tucked into the sloping landscape as if it had been there forever. My breath came in gasps as I gazed in wonder at the many buildings I saw beyond its outer wall.

The greatest of these, and what stood out most, was the kirk — a grand church, fourfold bigger than the one in our village. It rose from the surrounding hillside, as if it had been chiseled by the hammer of God Himself. It stretched as high as four of our huts, one stacked on top of the other, its spire like a finger that pointed straight to the heavens.

Smaller buildings sat clustered around the kirk. These were built of stone and thatch, like our homes, but they were enormous in comparison. And surrounding the whole of the property stood a great barricade of oak. With sharpened tips jutting skyward, it kept out any who thought to trespass. Staring toward the preceptory, I was hit with a longing to step inside the walls and disappear forever, to be one of them, to fight and have respect.

My palm was moist where it gripped the scroll. I took a breath and plunged on. The path was long and winding. It gave the watchers up on the barricade time to see any who might dare approach. My skin crept with the thought.

I was in a hurry and yet, in those last steps that led me to the place I had always wished to be, I hesitated. The gates were forbidding. They towered above me like mountains.

"What business have ye at this late hour?" A guard scowled down at me. His voice was like sand scraping my ears raw, and I ducked my head.

"I've come with a message for the Abbot. A Knight Templar bade me bring it." I twitched beneath the weight of his stare.

"Leave it in the hollow o' the stump over there by the rocks." He gestured to my left. "A runner will fetch it shortly." His voice dismissed me, and I heard him call out the order to someone within.

"No!" I shouted, panicked at the thought I'd come all this way only to be turned back at the gates. "I canno'." The protest started out strong, but my voice cracked piteously. I ducked my face to cover my embarrassment. "My instructions from the knight were very clear. I must deliver it personally." *Not the truth, o' course, but better.* I looked up, and he stepped closer to the wall's edge. His expression made me step back a pace.

A man must never slouch or flinch from the scrutiny o' another. This gives proof that ye're upright and speak the truth. It was as if my da were standing beside me, the thought came so clearly to my mind. I stood straighter and met the guard's eyes, feeling a bit of guilt for using my da's trick when I was lying. "Ye're wasting time," I said. Inwardly I cringed, willing the man to believe my ruse.

He left me to wait. I trembled as the wind skittered across my skin, wrapping my arms tight around me. The parchments crinkled beneath my fingers. *What am I doing? I should be in the village, warm by the fire.*

The silence of the night was broken suddenly by the squeal and clank of gears and winch. Slowly the gigantic gate began to rise and all of my misgivings fled.

My legs quaked and my eyes grew dry, but I refused to blink and miss a single moment. Templar preceptories were closed to the outside world. They were secret and silent. What went on beyond their walls was a mystery.

A DREAM REALIZED

The gate rose by agonizing degrees. Sound crept toward me long before I could see inside. I strained to hear, moving slowly toward the growing opening. The scrape of metal on metal was loud.

Unfolding before me was a scene I had only ever prayed to behold. Knights! Knights by the dozen were sparring. The hard-packed dirt clouded beneath their feet. I could taste the earth on my tongue and smell the sweat from their bodies.

They were training in groups of two or three. All wore mail from foot to helm. Some wore the brilliant white tunic with the red cross of the Templar Order. Others wore black with the same cross of red. In one hand they held large leather shields, and in the other enormous Scottish broadswords. I watched, dumfounded, as they beat each other mercilessly. The clash of blades filled the night air, each strike pounding so strongly I felt the resonance in my chest. I moved close, desperate to see.

"Follow me."

I jumped. The rasping command of the guard, who until recently was above the gate, was now so close to my ear that I nearly cried out.

"The Abbot will see ye."

His words were slow to enter my crowded head.

"Move, lad, or orders or no ye'll feel the flat o' my blade."

I followed him readily. I'd been on the receiving end of a belt and that was bad enough. His sword would leave marks for a sennight.

The guard led me along an old and well-used dirt path. We passed a host of buildings. The shutters of one were wide to the night air. Inside a blacksmith pounded a slab of hot metal before a brightly glowing forge. The guard prodded me forward.

A weaver's shed was next. As the smell of the dyes leached out into the night, my nose and eyes burned and I hurried past. Men were grinding wheat for flour in the next hut. We only had flour near on once a year. *What Mam could do with that . . .*

We crossed an open courtyard and came at last to the doors of the great kirk I had spied from my earlier vantage. The guard motioned that I should go first and herded me up a dark stone stairwell. It twisted several times before ending at a small wooden door.

The guard reached over me and knocked heavily. He was large — strong and close in the dark space. I thought again of the flat of his blade and tried to edge away, but there was no room on the small landing. From inside I heard the voices of men.

"As ye can see, the man's no' here. I have heard naught from him in more than a fortnight. Feel free to search the premises, but I can assure ye, yer efforts will be for naught." The deep voice was calm but forceful.

There was a slight pause and I leaned closer. "I'll take you at your word, Frère Abbot."

Danger seemed to hang in the air. I shifted back knowing that it would not do to be caught listening.

"Come," said the Abbot.

I could not see a latch or handle in the space before me, and while I grappled, the guard pushed from behind. The weight of my body forced the door to swing inward on hinges that squealed. I darted a sharp look behind me for the rough treatment. The guard neither met my eye nor acknowledged anything amiss. I inched forward, as much to put space between us as to see who was inside.

There were two large men in dark riding cloaks. They looked to have traveled hard and fast. A layer of road dust coated their legs and boots. A monk clad in brown homespun linen sat at a desk across from them. His hair was cut in the tonsure, an odd-looking thing where the sides were trimmed short and the very top circle of his head was shaved bald. His beard was full-faced but cut close to the chin. He was small, I noticed, barely inches over me, and I was only five hands high. He was as thin as a reed as well.

Throughout my inspection they all ignored me. The two soldiers — if I was not mistaken that that's what they were — stood, one by the Abbot's desk, the other by the high window.

The Abbot inclined his head. "Excuse me for a moment, gentlemen. Aye, lad?"

I stepped forward. "A Knight Templar gave this to me."

His eyes flashed with surprise, and before I could give over the scroll, one of the soldiers whipped it out of my hand. And though the Abbot protested, he broke the wax.

"Here, ye have no business —"

The soldier ignored him completely. "So you've heard nothing from him, Abbot," the man said scathingly as he looked over the document. "We'll just take this as evidence of his duplicity."

The Abbot fumed. "Ye have no right to intercept a Templar missive."

"Where it concerns a Templar wanted by the crown, we have every right." He turned to me. "Where did you get this, boy?"

His eyes were fierce and frightening. "A knight gave it to me two days past. I come from Berwick. He bade me bring it to the Abbot."

The soldier's cold and steady gaze raked me from head to foot. "Two days past, you say. You've come a long way from home."

I nodded, praying he believe me. I knew not why I lied, but for some reason my mind latched on to the point that these men were hunting the knight I had spoken to, and I had just made a fatal blunder in not getting the message in secret to the Abbot.

The lead man advanced on the Abbot with menace. "He will be found and brought to justice."

The Abbot ignored the taunt, addressing instead the guard behind me. "See them to the stables then out of the gates." He said nothing more.

I stood quietly as the door swung shut behind the men. "I'm sorry, I . . ."

He raised a finger quickly to his lips. My heart beat faster as I waited for his signal to resume speaking. It didn't come until the echo of the footsteps moved all the way down the stairs.

"Ye're a MacLeod, are ye not?" the Abbot asked.

How could he possibly know that?

"The resemblance to yer cousin Angus is remarkable," he said.

O' course. I'd forgotten Angus. His training was here. The Abbot would surely know him. Angus and I shared the same brilliant red hair and hazel eyes. It was a relief to think that I might turn out looking like Angus when a man. "Aye. He's my da's —"

"Ye're not from Berwick. What is this about?" he said with impatience.

"Aye, sir. I am from Leith, in the other direction. The knight arrived a' the croft before nightfall an' bade me come here an' tell no one. An' I did, sir, until just now." I felt badly about that.

I could see in his eyes the truth that I had made a very bad mistake. Then, just as I would have apologized, the room began to waver. I bit down hard on my cheek, willing the oddness creeping over me to recede. Light burst behind my eyes. *No!* I thought, *not here, not now!* It was coming, and I was helpless. The world seemed to slow to a crawl, as a dark hillside rose before my eyes and the smell of the ocean filled my nose. The sound of a battle echoed in my ears and still blue eyes stared lifelessly into mine.

"Lad, are ye unwell?" the Abbot asked with concern.

All at once the vision dropped away. I was back with a racing heart and sweat trickling down my neck.

"The Templar is in danger. There will be an ambush on the trader road by the sea." I didn't explain how I knew and the Abbot didn't ask. "He must be warned." I started for the door then turned back. "It was my fault."

He looked at me, worry in his eyes.

"I recognized the road. It snakes out to the sea. If he left directly after seeing me an' travels on horseback, he would have to go around the hills. I can go over them an' reach him sooner." I could not believe the words coming out of my mouth. And yet, the vision was so sharp in my mind I was terrified.

"It's late. Ye're a child. It's too dangerous an' ye should be home." He pushed back his stool, stood, and began to pace. "An' yet, the soldiers will be watching. If I send a contingent out a' this time o' night, they will surely notice an' follow."

His eyes narrowed and he looked at me closely. "Ye know the way, well an' truly?" he asked.

"Aye, sir. I will reach him. Ye can rely on me."

He came to a decision then. Taking out a clean bit of parchment, he penned a message. "This missive must be delivered only into the hands o' the knight. 'Tis a matter o' life that I entrust to ye, lad. I will see that ye're rewarded for yer efforts."

But Da will already be furious, I thought. *Am I mad? The strapping will be bad.* And yet, the Abott's eyes were bright with encouragement. "I will do it, sir. But will ye assure the family that I am well?" They still expected me at the bonfire. This was no quick trip over the hillside. "Perhaps . . ." I hesitated.

"Aye?" he asked.

"Do ye think ye could see fit to sending my mam just a bit o' flour?"

"Aye, lad. O' course. It will be taken care o'. Here. Take this for yer own troubles. Be careful. Be swift." He dropped several coppers into my hand and stepped beyond the door, calling for a guard. I squeezed the coins, fretting. The guard popped his head in. "See that a pack is readied in the kitchens. Two days' fare," the Abbott said. The man disappeared quickly.

"Stop by the kitchen on yer way. 'Tis down those stairs an' through the corridor to yer left. Speak to no one. Not here. Not on the road. Go with haste, lad." He laid his hand upon my head and made the cross on my forehead. "Go with God."

RUN WITH THE WIND

What have I done? I left beneath the full dark of the night sky. I could scarcely believe the Abbot had agreed I should make the trip. An odd sense of moving in a dream hung over me. On the one hand I felt the urgent need to find and warn the knight. But I also felt guilt and worry that my family, by now, must be wondering what happened to me. It would take a while for a runner to reach the hut to tell of my errand, and even longer to find my family still at the festival in the village. Unless . . . unless they were worried when I had not shown up and were, even now, hunting the woods looking for signs of my passage. "Please hurry," I whispered to the faceless messenger.

For my part, I ran from the moment I left the preceptory, sometimes fast, sometimes not quite as quickly. It depended on the terrain. Scotia, and in particular this stretch of land I traveled, was a maze of hills and vales. I knew them like I knew my own name. My direction remained true to my inner compass — and yet my spine tingled. Everyone knew that spirits walked abroad in the dark, waiting to ambush unwary souls and drag them off to the underworld. There were certain days of the year when that was more a possibility than others. Tonight was one of those nights.

Beltane. It was the time when the veil between the dead and the undead grew thin. Much as I would have liked to forget that bit of information, it hung around in my mind, popping out at every wavering shadow and rattle of branches. My fingers sketched the ward against evil as I ran: thumb, pointer, pinky, all pointed toward the earth.

Even more frightening, I heard a cry in the night. There was no mistaking it — wolves — a pack from the sound of it. Their howls rent the darkness with an eerie, inhuman wail. The Devil was hunting abroad.

I ran faster. Tales of evil, voracious man-wolves who traveled with the Devil were Torquil's favorite way to frighten me.

It was hard to figure from which direction they would come. Their cries echoed off the hillsides: first before me, then behind. Keeping to the flat, marshy wetlands, I bolted, staying low and silent on the moors between the hills.

The wind blew strong on my face. Ordinarily it would not have been long before the pack scented me, but the rains had been heavy for much of a fortnight. The rivers and small, trickling burns were swelled, and the ground was spongy beneath my feet. My boots were wet and I could not run very quickly, but I was glad of the earth's fullness. The deep mossy smell did much to cover my scent.

I traveled the bogs for more than a candle mark with a long, loping stride that was far from comfortable. When finally I cleared their uneven surface and hit flat-packed earth, I settled into a steady pace. It was good, not having to be constantly aware of my footing. My tread was light, my breathing regular. The sound of the wolf pack faded and my mind wandered.

I imagined the look on Torquil's face when he heard that I had been chosen as a Templar messenger. My mam would be fearful, knowing I was out unprotected in the night. I asked God to give her peace and also to make my da forget to beat me for delaying the Beltane festival.

Mostly, though, I thought about the map. It was of no place that was familiar to me. Though I knew nothing of the printed word, I was certain that the writing was scribed in a foreign tongue. It bore no resemblance to our native Gaelic. The landmarks on the map were strange, compelling shapes. I traced them with a finger in my mind as I ran, remembering them as if they were still strongly before me. The land's edge. The mountains. The waterfall.

It was the dead still of night when I came on the pass. I was up in the hills overlooking the beginning of the road that led out to the sea. There was no sign of the Templar, so I made my way down to an outcropping of rocks to settle in and wait.

I dug some dried beef from my pack and washed it down with water from the skin the Abbot had provided. In the pack was also some bread and cheese. We didn't get bread often at home. We ate mostly bannock cakes of oat and water. In moments I was full and sleepy. I'd only ever stayed up when helping bring in the sheep. It was late and I had been on the run for a good long time.

The rocks I sat on were cold, but I was far too tired to stand. Though my body shivered, I found myself drifting off every few moments. Each time I caught myself, I jerked awake with a start. I could not afford to miss the knight. When my body adjusted to the hard seat and it grew comfortable, I forced myself to stand and pace. When that was not enough, I entertained myself by redrawing the map, both in my mind and with a twig in the dirt at my feet.

I sat again finally, for in truth I couldn't keep upright. I dreamt then of a great flow of water crashing down over a mountain of rock.

The clop of horses echoed among the hills, and I woke suddenly.

A MESSAGE DELIVERED

I leapt to my feet. I couldn't see well. It might be the knight, but he was not alone. I opened my mouth as if to shout, but before I did the lead man slowed. I darted behind the rock as he turned his mount and scanned the hills. All at once his eyes fixed on me.

"Lad, come!" he called.

I hurried down the incline. "How did ye know to look for me? In the darkness how could ye see?" I sputtered. My breath came in short bursts.

"It matters not. How come ye to be here, little man?"

"Tormod!" I said with exasperation. "My name is Tormod. I bring word from the Abbot. There is an ambush set somewhere in the hills on the road to the sea." I handed him the scroll with the vision of what I'd seen fresh in my mind.

The Templar turned into the light of the moon, split the seal, and unraveled the parchment. He read the message rapidly; I saw his shock.

"The lad speaks true. The Abbot urges us to avoid the pass and seek the Archbishop Lambert at Dover Castle. Soldiers from France have been to the preceptory looking for us. They have taken the map." The Templar motioned his group toward a dense clump of trees by the side of the road. *The pass*, I thought. *Aye. 'Tis good that ye not go there.* I knew not when or precisely where the ambush would take place, but I was still certain the fight was coming.

The thought bothered me. I turned away, studying the men in his complement. There were five: the Templar, a soldier, two monks, and an old man.

"France. Could they be from the Pope?" asked one of the monks.

"Papal soldiers rarely set foot beyond the residence," said the soldier. "We have to assume others." He scanned the landscape. "The pass is the only way in and out o' these hills." He was, I estimated, about seventeen winters. He was tall, six hands for sure. His body was wiry, and not yet as muscular as the knights I had seen training, but he was on his way to becoming strong. His hair was a golden blond, and his eyes were bluish green. He wore the colors of a trainee: a black linen tunic with the cross of red, like my cousin Angus. He noticed my scrutiny and stared back, his eyes flicking over my thin form. It was a look I was used to.

"Aye, Seamus, 'tis the only road, but we dare no' use it." The knight had dismounted and signaled the others to do so as well. From a skin bag that had been hanging from his saddle he watered his horse. The sergeant, Seamus, checked the hooves of his own mount. I sat on a rock by the knight, puzzling over the conversation I had just heard. The rest of the company spread out, taking their rest nearby.

"Do we still try for the ship?" the monk nearest me asked. He was a small, round man with a red face and a nervous energy. He plucked at his robes and adjusted his seat several times before standing once again.

"Aye, Brother Callum. There is no' another due this way for many a day. We dare no' tarry," said the knight.

"Neither do we dare go through the pass an' put ourselves at risk," replied the second monk. He was a sharp contrast to the first. His voice was deep and seemed almost rusted, as if he used it infrequently. He was moderately sized, with a thin frame and the meek look of someone who preferred solitude to people. Still, he took some bannocks from his pack and offered them to me. I declined. I still had food in my pack that I had yet to investigate, but when he held out a skin of water I took it gratefully.

"There has to be another way through these hills," the Templar muttered, stroking the muzzle of his mount.

"We thank ye, child, for bringing the message," said the peaceful monk. "I am Andrus an' this is Douglas." The monk motioned to the old man beside him. He was wiry and withered, and yet he seemed strong and able. "Over there as ye heard is Callum, an' that is Seamus." He pointed to the other men in turn.

"I am Tormod," I said, nodding to the nearest.

"Ye traveled long. Ye must be tired," said the one called Andrus.

"I am well," I said. "I am my da's runner. I am used to delivering messages. I know these hills and the shortest routes for travel." Suddenly I knew I had the answer they sought.

"Sir Knight, I know a way," I said, climbing to my feet and moving to his side. "There are trails that wind up through the hills an' around the pass. I can lead ye. I'll not lie. 'Tis not an easy trek an' much o' it must be done afoot. The horses will have to be led. But it can be done."

Seamus protested. "Alex, what can he know? He's but a lad."

The mighty Templar's eyes assessed me then. "Aye. An' were it no' for this balach, we would have ridden to our deaths this very day."

The thought troubled me, almost as much as his calling me a lad. The vision, never far from my thoughts, loomed in my mind.

"Have any o' ye a better idea?" the Templar asked.

Seamus turned away. The others shook their heads no.

"Ye're sure o' this, little ma . . . Tormod?" He was not outwardly skeptical, but I could tell if there were another way he would consider it instead and this gave me pause.

Could I do it? "Aye. 'Tis the path o' the drovers. I have walked it many a time."

At his signal they gathered around and he told the plan. I watched the reactions on their faces. Most were receptive. Seamus was openly against it, but he was overruled by the Templar.

"Brother Callum, I must rely on ye to ride back and assure the Abbot the message was delivered successfully."

The Templar's eyes flickered over me, assessing. My stomach grew tight. "The rest o' us will go on as planned, with a bit o' a deviation that I pray will turn out right." He took the reins of his mount, and with a look around to make sure the others were ready, said, "Come, Tormod. Lead us."

THE PATH OF AVOIDANCE

We had to retrace a bit of the way I had come to them, but within the candle mark we had picked up the trail I remembered. It was a thin and winding track that wove up the slope and through the scrub. My da, the boys, and I had helped clear it over the past two autumns, helping our neighbors take their herd this way after losing several head to raiders in the pass.

I was awake, but the feeling of moving in a dream was strong. My eyes were gritty from lack of sleep, and my legs felt as if they didn't belong to me. The men spoke among themselves. The soft buzz of their conversation hummed in my ears. The Templar said little. He seemed content to walk with me, though his eyes never settled overlong on any one thing. His vigilance was constant. Had I to watch our trail ahead, the hills beside, and our back as well, I could not have managed it all. I had trouble enough making sure the track I sought in the moonlight was the correct one.

"Tell me, Tormod. How did the Abbot seem? Did he say any more to ye than what ye mentioned already?"

His voice took me by surprise. I glanced sharply up at him, scarcely believing not only that he would speak to me, but also that he would ask an opinion. "No. The soldiers were there with him when I arrived. The Abbot told them ye were not there and said if they didn't believe him, they could search the place. But . . ."

He looked at me expectantly. "Aye?" he asked.

"I knew they would not."

"Why?"

"He seemed powerful, my Lord Knight, as if it would somehow be a trespass they would regret." I knew I was not making a whole lot of sense.

"Powerful?" he asked.

"Aye." I said. "Not a' first, for the Abbot seemed small, ye know, but when he spoke, it was with such authority, I knew they, and I, would do anything he asked. Something strong seemed to come from the man.

I knew that if he commanded, I would obey. It's like with my da, but more so — though if ye should ever meet him, I'd ask ye not to mention that."

A small smile played about his mouth. I waited for him to speak more, but he went back to his silent ways.

We had walked a mark of the candle. My legs were beyond weary, and I felt as if I slept as I moved. And yet the night was barely begun. The others didn't seem bothered by the travel. Ahead was the highest peak we would have to cross. It was tough on the horses, and the men were busy both calming and coaxing them upward. I was trying to work up the courage to speak to the Templar without him speaking to me first.

I was leading the way and very nearly to the top of the heights when his arm reached out and snagged my plaid. "Stop here," he said softly. He motioned all of us to silence. To the one, each man dropped to a crouch as he, already low, scrambled silently to the cliff's edge and peered down into the blackness.

"What is it?" I whispered, appearing at his elbow uninvited.

His glare stopped my heart and stilled my tongue, and he yanked me from my crouch down flat onto my stomach.

Peering down, I didn't see them at first, but one chose that moment to dart from a clump of scrub. Men were scattered along the hillside behind clusters of rock, lying among patches of gorse. Their attention was focused on the path below.

"Do we attack?" I whispered tightly.

"No. Not unless we have no other choice. We do not shed blood lightly, Tormod," he whispered. Slowly he backed away from the ridge and signaled that I should do the same.

"They would have no second thoughts to killing ye," I mumbled.

He addressed me solemnly. "Death comes to all, but I do not hasten any toward it. We are outnumbered in man, strength, and arms. My mission is o' great importance. It canno' be abandoned for foolishness."

I nodded, chastened, and rose to a crouch, ready to make my way back down. Yet, as I stood I was suddenly hit by a wave of unsteadiness. It had been rough travel and I had risen too quickly. I felt myself lose balance and begin to fall. A shower of rock clattered along with me.

From beyond the rise, I heard them.

"Take cover!" the Templar cried.

The sound of men swarming over the hill overtook me, yet I could do nothing but tumble and slide down the rocky hillside. I hit my head and tore my hands trying to stop my descent and only slowed near the bottom. My head was pounding as I crawled behind a group of rocks. A trickle of blood ran down into my eye, and I rubbed it away trying to see what was happening.

The Templar and his men ranged on the slope above me. Brother Andrus and Douglas had moved behind trees and drawn their bows. The Templar and Seamus made a wall at the top of the hill, and for a moment there was no movement or sound but the clatter of stone and the war cry of the approaching men.

Turning back to back, the Templar and Seamus lifted their swords. Almost as one, their words rang clear. *"Non nobis, Domine."*

And it began.

The first man came over the rise not expecting a frontal attack. The Templar swung mightily, and I gasped. The blade cut deep. The man staggered and went down with a scream that curdled my blood. The next man was right behind, another and still another. The scene was mad. I could barely follow the many things that were happening. Seamus had engaged two, and as they fell another came toward him bent on death. An arrow suddenly embedded itself in the attacker's shoulder and his sword merely glanced Seamus's mail. Brother Andrus was notching and firing arrows at a rate I could barely credit. And Douglas . . . Douglas I saw reached for an arrow only to find his quiver empty.

The blood in my veins turned to ice. I knew what was going to happen. With a sick lurch I stood, shouting to make him see and understand. "Douglas, get down!"

It was almost a dream, a horrible, revolting night-mare. *My vision.* I closed my eyes to shut it away. Yet the image remained before the brightness of my mind. I saw the sharp, black arrow pierce the fragile white throat. Blood, dark and crimson, surged around the shaft. I saw him stagger back, fall, and begin the roll downhill.

Something snapped deep inside me and I opened my eyes, my mind rearing away as I scrambled on my knees from my place of safety toward Douglas. "No," I cried. The blood from the wound on his neck trickled to the ground beneath his head. *I caused this to happen.*

My fingers began to throb unexpectedly. Heat washed over me, and the tingling feel of a legion of ants ran along a path inside me. I stared at the back of my open hand, uncomprehending, and the man beneath my fingers moved. His eyes fluttered, opened, and seized upon mine. I saw wonder in them, and then they drifted closed and his body became still. I slumped back on the rough, rocky ground and darkness took me.

GUILT AND REPARATION

"Tormod. Can ye hear me?"

The Templar's voice was far away, and I was so very

tired and heartsore that it took much to heed his call. He was persistent, however, far more than I could ignore. I opened my eyes a sliver and moaned at the shaft of pain the light brought to my head.

"Aye, lad. Stay awake. Look into my eyes."

I did, but it hurt like the very devil. "I'm sorry," I said. "I am so very sorry." I could not help the tears that leaked from the edges of my eyes, however much they mortified me. He thought their cause was the pain of my injury, but it was the dead, sightless eyes of Douglas haunting my mind.

" 'Tis over, Tormod. Ye've been hurt in yer fall, but naught is broken, I think. Can ye sit?"

"The others . . ."

He ferreted my meaning and then knew my thoughts well and truly. There was a terrible sadness in his eyes. "We are safe."

I understood the thing he didn't say. I knew that the old man had passed on, and yet still I had hoped. I turned my head, though the pain nearly broke me in two, and was sick in the dirt. A man was dead, because I had been careless. There was no getting around that.

"He was old, Tormod, an' lived a long, full life. It was the way he would have wanted to go. It was no' yer fault."

I could not meet his eyes. I would believe him in all, save that, for I knew better. I turned away only to see a pile of dead and bloodied bodies. I fought back the bile. I had wanted a conflict, to fight as a Templar. Yet it was nothing like I had envisioned.

"Come, Seamus, help me lift him."

Seamus came at the Templar's call, and I had the wish then that he had been the one to take the message to the Abbot. Seamus was angry and made it known.

Roughly he drew me to a sitting position. My world swayed as my head pulsed. The Templar interceded. "There are horses wandering below. Get them; we've lost two." His mouth was an angry line, and his voice was that of the superior, strong and not to be questioned. "We must no' delay, and Tormod canno' walk the rest o' the way while injured."

"He should go back," Seamus brooded. "We have no need o' a guide. The road is below, and we can pass unmolested. The balach should go home." Before he turned away, he raked a black gaze over me.

"Aye. His place is home," said the Templar. "But as we canno' afford the time to bring him, nor send him injured and alone on his way, he stays." His words raised my spirits a little.

Seamus spun around, his eyes wide with surprise. "Ye mean to take him with us?"

The Templar's strange assessing gaze was on me again. "At least as far as the coast. We can arrange an

escort to see him home. Go, Seamus. Do as I said."
Seamus turned away and disappeared over the hill.

As far as the coast. I was disappointed deep inside. I
had not really expected that I should become one of
them, but perhaps in a corner of my mind the possibility
had taken root. I stood on my own, though I teetered
with dizziness. "I am well enough."

The Templar caught me as I swayed. "Ye're strong
o' heart, Tormod, but yer body is injured. 'Tis nothing o' which to be ashamed. The enemy is gone for the
moment. We continue our journey through the pass
an' hope there are no others hunting us. 'Tis urgent we
move quickly or I'd give ye more time to recover. Can ye
ride, lad?"

"Aye. I'll not hold ye up." I tried to keep my head
still as I spoke though every movement sent sparks of
pain through me. At the corner of my vision, I saw the
rocks the men had gathered for the cairn of Douglas.
Tears filmed my eyes, and I blinked them away. It was
hard to swallow. Brother Andrus put his hand on my
back as he passed by.

"Ye will ride with me for now," said the Templar.
"There are four horses, two stronger than the rest.
Seamus and I will take turns carrying ye so as not to tire
the mounts unduly." I hoped we would reach the coast
quickly. Seamus had no use for me, and though I could

see that he would not disobey any direct command from the knight, nothing demanded that he be pleasant about dispatching his duty.

I sat and watched as the men piled the rocks over the body. I wanted to help them, but the pounding in my head made it difficult to move.

I looked at my hands. They were scratched and torn from my fall. I stretched and folded them, staring but not seeing. Then something about them struck a memory I had forgotten. I thought of the strange tingling that had gone through them. I thought of the heat and the last stirring of Douglas.

"He could help," Seamus grumbled as he added the last rock to the pile. His voice pulled me from my thoughts and I stood. A wave of nausea tilted through me, but I shook it off and approached the grave. The Templar began to pray and the others joined in. When they got to a part I knew, I added my voice. Seamus bristled. I could feel his anger crossing the space between us.

INJURY

We rode steadily, chasing the moon across the night sky. The wind had picked up as we moved through the pass, bringing with it the salty scent of the sea. Each foot forward of our mount was a penance I paid for the death I knew I had caused. And though it was much deserved, and I should have accepted it as my due, my traitorous, wretched mind prayed for the road's quick end.

It was a wonder that I was able to stay astride. It was much to the credit of the knight who held me before him. Even when it came time to switch me over to the sergeant, the Templar arranged to merely trade horses, sensing no doubt the other's feelings on it.

To my head's aching dismay, the knight kept a soft but running dialogue between us, urging my participation. "Tell me about yer life here, Tormod."

I shrugged, though regretted the movement as pain threatened to split my skull. "What is there to tell?" I said softly. "My life is naught but fishing an' family. Yer life is adventure with strange places an' amazing sights." I closed my eyes, preferring the darkness to the bright that hurt. I wanted and needed sleep, but he seemed determined to keep me from it.

"Adventure is a misleading thing, Tormod. It covers naught o' the pain an' guilt, uncertainty an' fear."

Fear, I thought, *how can one such as he be fearful o' anything?* The guilt I now knew firsthand, but I detected sadness in him as well. I began to tell him of the village, my family, and the celebration I had missed. He seemed to relax in the hearing.

"I kept ye from that," he said. "I ask yer pardon."

I twisted in surprise. It hurt something awful and I swayed. His big hand grasped the drape of plaid across my chest, and he hauled me upright. "Ye need ask nothing o' me. I've longed to be gone from there."

He remained quiet, perhaps assuming that I would explain my words, but I could not. How could I tell him that every day was a trial there, that I was looked on even in my own home as an oddity. I pushed aside the memory that haunted me.

"My mam will be worried," I said.

"The Abbot will assure them that ye're well."

I must have tensed for he read something in my manner.

"What?" His voice rumbled in my ear.

I was afraid to even voice my thoughts. "I was on my way to deliver the flint an' tinder for starting the Beltane bonfire when ye arrived. I didn't deliver the supplies. I just left. Do ye think that God will punish us if the Beltane ceremonies didn't start as planned?"

The livelihood of the whole village depended on the season's catch. If I had angered God, would He prevent a fruitful season?

He was quiet a moment, thinking on his reply. "God is not a vengeful being. Whether or not the Beltane fire was lit on time is not a reason He would punish a village. The catch will depend on the weather, the feeding cycles o' the fish, an' about a dozen other factors."

I was shocked to hear him speak so. Da was adamant on the doctrine that all of the ancient holy days be observed just so. But the Templar's words were confident. I wanted to believe him, even if it was just that I didn't want to worry over the possibility of one more bad thing happening because of me. I almost had more guilt and worry than I could deal with.

"Well, I'll be strapped for it either way." I said. It didn't worry me as much as it might. I didn't look forward to it, and it would hurt, but I would get over it within a day. To me, it was worth it to be here now. To have seen what I had and been a small part of their complement for even a short time.

"Will it be bad?" the Templar asked.

I cringed thinking on it.

"Not overmuch," I said. "But he reminded me twice today that I was responsible for the fire. I paid him no mind, because Torquil had agreed to do it."

"Why should ye be strapped then?" he asked.

"Because I trusted my brother," I said bitterly. "I traded a portion o' his duty hauling wood for running back to the croft to get the materials. He reneged on the arrangement."

"Ye will tell your da that happened?"

"I don't know. It was my responsibility. I should not have tried to trade it away in the first place. Mam gets worked up when there are punishments. An' she is with child."

"Yer mam is strong," the Templar said. "An' ye will set it to right with yer brother."

I didn't reply. There were times when I wondered if things would ever be set to right between Torquil and me.

"If ye would," I said softly. "Tell me where ye've been an' what ye've seen. I canno' talk anymore. I have not slept all night. My head aches something fierce."

"The ship is not long away. Sleep. I will keep ye upright. I don't believe yer head injury to be serious. 'Tis why I kept ye awake. To check it. We'll talk later."

I gave in, gratefully. And drifted into oblivion.

TAKEN

I came awake in bits and starts during the rest of the trek. The hills around us were deeply shadowed. The heather, a vibrant purple by day, was barely brighter than the rocks and road by moonlight.

On waking, the Templar passed me a strong drink from a skin. Its taste was odd, like berries, bark, and wood smoke. I didn't like it very much, but it seemed to make the blistering ache in my head go away. I must have slept again after drinking it, for I don't remember more of the trip.

I came to when I felt the horse beneath me stop and the Templar slide from his place. My head was thick and my mouth was rotted and dry. "Where are we?" I mumbled.

The Templar hissed for silence, and the strong grip he laid on my arm brought me awake fast. We were at the top of a rise, hidden by a copse of dense trees. Below was the sea. The rhythmic wash of waves beat in my blood and made the night seem alive and dangerous.

I knew to heed the Templar's warning this time. There was an urgency in his bearing I recognized. Quietly I slid from our mount, grabbing the saddle to steady myself. The Templar pulled up his cloak to cover his silver hood of mail and without a word slipped silently away. I watched, tense under the onslaught of a stiff breeze that whipped the hillside. His silhouette was dark, the black of his cloak nearly concealing him. He angled down toward the beach and I lost sight of him. Still staring down to the beach, I tied off our mount.

Seamus and Brother Andrus hung back in the shadow of the trees.

In the small harbor, an enormous ship rocked gently in the wash. It was a cog, a single-masted merchant ship, with curved outer planking at the sides of its hull. High on the single sail, the red Templar cross blazed in the moonlight. I had seen these ships in our harbor many times and watched as the cargo had been loaded and unloaded.

Two men stood sentinel on the small rocky beach. I had not seen them at first, for they carried no torches and blended with the darkness, but their voices carried over the wind.

The language was different than my own, a murmur that was nearly muffled by the surf. At my side the leaves stirred suddenly, and my heart lodged itself somewhere behind my tongue. The Templar moved past me to Seamus.

"Our ship has been taken," the Templar said softly.

"Who are they?" Seamus asked.

"More o' the same from the pass," said the Templar.

"What do they want?" I asked, though it earned me a dark look from Seamus.

The Templar answered plainly, "Apparently they want me."

"The odds are not in our favor, Alex," Seamus said. "There are two on the shore an' a' least one prowls the deck. We don't know if there are more below or if others were sent ashore to seek us out." His voice was filled with doubt, but I heard resignation as well. "We will take it back." It was not a question but a conclusion.

The Templar did not hesitate. "Aye. 'Tis our only hope. We must be gone from here."

"Aye," said the sergeant. "Ye have a plan?" My mind reeled trying to understand the conversation.

"Not much o' one, but better than none. I'll swim out from the east point. 'Tis not far from the prow. There is a rope that anchors the ship on that side. I will go up it."

I swallowed hard imagining such a maneuver.

"I'll need a diversion on the shore, something to draw the watch away from that side."

"I shall give ye one," said Seamus, reaching out. They clasped each other's forearms.

"May the Lord guide our steps with light," said the Templar.

"An' our faith remain true," replied Seamus.

The hair on my arms stood on end. The Templar turned away and started down the slope. I followed. My tread was not as silent as his was. He turned suddenly and motioned me back. I shook my head no. He glared and pointed back again, then turned and continued down the hill without another glance.

I hesitated, but for only a moment, then followed

him down the incline. He knew I was there, but refused to acknowledge my open disobedience. I moved as he moved, crouched when he crouched. I thought about the fall I had taken and the consequences of it and paid close attention to my footing. I would not — could not — repeat the incident and cause the Templar any more trouble.

When we reached the rocks by the jetty, he shed his cloak and vestments.

"Ye need someone at yer back," I murmured.

Though he was not speaking to me, I reached for his cloak. I could feel his annoyance. "I just mean to fold it for ye," I whispered meekly.

He was not happy with me, but let me take the garment as he took off his mail and dropped it beside his boots and sword. In tunic and breeks he moved toward the water.

"Would ye no' be faster in yer braies," I whispered. The smaller underclothes would be easier to swim in.

As he stepped into the water he said, " 'Tis forbidden." I looked after him, puzzled. I must have been mistaken in my hearing. *Forbidden*, I thought, *to swim in yer braies in the ocean? How strange. Forbidden by whom? And why?* I could not ask as he was up to his waist by then.

The Templar was a good swimmer and the ocean

water was calm. I watched, breathing in time to the movement of his body as it dipped beneath the water. Then when I could bear the tension no more I turned away.

His clothes were piled on the rock beside me. I picked up his mantle. It was fine cloth, soft and tightly woven. Beneath were the hard links of iron that made up his mail. The loops rippled beneath my fingers, and when I lifted it, I was amazed at its heaviness and the way it was both hard and fluid at the same time. I lowered the mail to the rock to see what more was there. A glint of silver and flash of jewels made me gasp — a dagger! I wondered where he had kept it. The sheath had a cloth tie worked through its top. He must have had it tied to his arm.

In the half-light I lifted the knife, awed by its foreign beauty. The haft was silver and etched with many birds and animals. Their eyes were studded with glistening jewels that seemed to wink as I turned and admired them. The blade was not made in Scotia. I knew it came from the far-off, from the land of the Saracens.

Reverently I slid the knife from its sheath and rested the edge on the pad of my thumb. The quick jab of pain as the blade cut took me by surprise.

I looked up quickly. The Templar was nearly halfway to the ship. The knife glinted in my hand. My body tensed. He was unarmed.

UNARMED

I threw off my plaid, tunic, and breeks as fast as I could. *He was unarmed. Did he forget the knife?* The thought seemed to rattle inside my head. I stumbled down the dark and slippery rocks, determined to reach him in time. Barnacles tore at my feet, but I ignored them and hurried into the ocean.

The water was freezing. I clenched my teeth to still their chattering. My hands were instantly numb, and when I began to stroke, the knife was hard to hold.

I was a stronger swimmer than the knight, even with an aching head and sore body. The sea and I were long friends. I skimmed the waves and let the current do much to pull me out, but he'd reached the ship before I could catch him. There was no way to get his attention. His hands were on the anchor's rope. I stopped stroking and floated, lifting the knife above the water.

Suddenly, he turned and fixed a glare directly at me. Cold as I was, the eerie way he seemed to sense my presence made my shivering multiply tenfold. The scowl on his face, however, told me right off how angry he was that I had followed.

From the shore came the sound of an argument. It was Seamus. His words were overloud and quite unlike his usual serious tones. It sounded, I thought, like several of our crew when they've dipped overmuch into the ale.

"This is the ship I paid passage for, an' a good lot o' silvers it was, too," said Seamus. "They told me to be here a' the rise o' the moon, an' I am. Step aside an' let me by." His voice seemed to float across the water.

The silhouette of the Templar was black against the darkness of the ship's hull. Slowly he made his way, hand over hand, nearly silently up the rope. I watched him go over the rail and out of sight.

On the shore, Seamus was still arguing.

"What goes on there?" A strong, deep voice cut the night directly above me where the Templar had gone over. I held my breath.

"A drunkard," the man from on shore replied.

"Kill him," the one on deck commanded.

A clash of blades and muffled oaths crossed the water. Frantic, I glided toward the ship. Something was happening there as well.

What should I do? The whole of my body was trembling with cold and fear, but suddenly I decided. I stuck the knife between my teeth, reached for the rope, and began to climb.

It was more difficult than I had reckoned. The

Templar made it seem easy, but my body was wet and my arms ached beneath the strain. I tried to set my mind to other climbs, other times when I'd scaled the hut walls to reach the roof to do the thatching repairs. But never had the hut pitched beneath the roll of waves.

The sound of a scuffle grew loud as I neared the rail. My mouth was tight, holding the knife in my teeth, and my throat was dry. My legs shook and my arms burned as I pulled myself up and over, fearful that I would be seen, terrified that an assassin waited there to kill me.

The deck was black, but the silhouette of two men was clear. I scrambled behind a pile of sailcloth palming the knife as I went.

The Templar faced an opponent much larger than he. The man was enormous, and in his gigantic arms a broadsword gleamed. Yet neither man moved.

As I stared, I slowly became aware of a strange itch in the back of my mind, the movement of something behind my eyes and deep within my ears.

I shook my head to clear it, but the oddity remained. Then from my place I heard what I hadn't before — the soft sound of the Templar's voice.

"How did ye know I was here?"

His assailant's murmur was too low for me to catch.

"Where is the map taken from the Abbot?"

Again the other spoke, but I could make out nothing.

I moved closer. Listening hard. Nothing came to me. Frustrated, I leaned forward. Suddenly the mounded material I was leaning on began to slip. I couldn't stop myself; I pitched forward and the knife clattered loudly to the deck.

Immediately something seemed to snap and change around me. The attacker roared and swung his blade. The Templar dodged and spun, then, where moments before his hands had been empty, two palm-sized cross daggers glinted. Without pause he threw both — one to the heart, one between the eyes.

The attacker's sword wavered and a strange gurgle wheezed from his lips. I gasped. Shock and pain filled his eyes. Blood poured from his wounds, and yet I could not look away from him. The Templar quickly stepped aside and, as I watched, the man pitched forward.

All at once the night was still.

The Templar approached the dead man and removed his knives. Hurriedly he wiped them clean, then kneeling, he whispered a soft prayer, closed the man's eyes, lifted the body, and dropped him over the rail.

It was as if I felt the hungry waves reach up and accept their bounty.

"Are there others?" I whispered, unable to keep my eyes from the rail where the man had disappeared.

"Only on the beach." He moved past me, looking toward shore. The fight there was over. Seamus and Brother Andrus were in a small skin boat and nearly on us.

"Lower the rope for them. I must go below and see to the crew." As he turned away, he hesitated a moment, and then his soft voice filled the space between us. "Ye put yerself in harm's way, Tormod. If ye have no regard for yer own life, next time consider the lives o' others."

He was very angry with me. Without a backward glance, he went below.

I turned away and dropped the ladder. The swish as it hit the water reminded me of the sound the body made after it went over the rail. My stomach twisted suddenly, and I was horrified to feel what was left inside rush up. It nearly hit Seamus as he climbed from the coracle.

"Watch it, rat!" he hissed.

God's breath? What did I do? Sick with worry and confusion, I stumbled back from the rail and folded to the deck, wrapping my arms around my knees. The Templar came up from below, and I watched him as unobtrusively as I could. Seamus met him at the top of the ladder.

"Are either o' the two ashore alive?" the Templar asked.

"No," Seamus replied. "But they were from Philippe." He held out something small for the Templar's inspection.

"Aye. The brooch shows his crest. We must be gone from here now. There may be more on the way. Danger is high. We leave on the next tide, but we have a problem." I felt his eyes rest on me. "We don't have the luxury o' sending Tormod back."

Not go back? I thought. *Aye, please let me stay.*

"Not send him back?" Seamus was filled with amazement. "Ye must be mad. He's a disadvantage. We'll have to watch over him every moment. Why would ye do that?"

I looked daggers at Seamus but he didn't even notice.

The Templar was silent a moment before he spoke. It was with a tone I had not heard from him thus far. "I have seen it, Seamus. Our meeting was destined. There is a part this one will play."

Surprise rushed through me. *He'd seen it. . . . How? And, what could he mean? He was angry with me. I did things that were wrong. A part to play. What part?*

Seamus looked ready to disagree but held his tongue. The Templar stepped then to the rail and raised his face to the waning light of the moon. I read many things there — not the half of which frightened me terribly — but strongest was the sense of desperation, of a man seeking hope in the faintest of places.

In me? I dropped my head onto my arms, praying for the ship to leave, to hurry and take me into a new life of adventure.

PART TWO

CONFRONTATION

The splash of the waves against the ship was the only break in the silence of morning. A cold mist wafted across the deck. I was freezing and pulled the blanket someone had laid over me tighter. Bits and pieces of the night came back as I came fully awake. The memories seemed a part of some other life, not mine. So much had happened. My throat was dry and my body ached. And then out of nowhere a rush of excitement filled me. I was still here. The ship had sailed. I was with them!

But then, as if something warned me not to get too happy, his words came back. *If ye have no regard . . .* I pushed them away. *He said I had a part to play. I'll just have to make it up to him.* I smiled. For the first time in many days I had something to look forward to. *No one to order me about, no bairns, no sheep. No explanation needed for the things I could do or the things that happened when I was around.* My grin was wide. The Templar had been truly angry with me for disobeying him, but he hadn't sent me home. I would try very hard not to do anything foolhardy again.

The sun was well above the horizon. Water surrounded the ship. The air was sharp and cold. I shivered, drawing my knees close. My tunic, trews, plaid, and sporran lay in a pile at my elbow. The jeweled dagger lay atop them. I'd have to give it back. Quickly, I dressed, glad of the warmth, and went in search of the Templar.

At the door of the forecastle, I paused. Something stopped me from entering directly, perhaps the hushed tone of the voices inside.

"If they got to the Pope, could they no' have gotten to the Archbishop?" I heard Seamus ask.

"Aye. But we must take the chance. The Archbishop has to be told o' the treachery. De Nogaret must answer for his crimes. We're being hunted, an' Philippe's men have the map. We need an intermediary to go to Pope Clement," said the Templar. His voice had dropped to an urgent whisper. "The Archbishop will send someone."

"'Tis too dangerous. Why do we not go straight to the Grand Master?"

"He has already left for a tour of the European preceptories. I dare not step on French soil without allies, Seamus." The Templar's voice was not to be questioned. "We go to the Archbishop as the Abbot instructed, an' rendezvous with Ahram by month's end in Spain, where we will seek out the Grand Master. He's due to see the

62

Spanish Templars in June. If we miss him an' he's gone on to France, Ahram will give us an armed escort there."

Neither said anything for a moment. I leaned closer to the door and the floorboard creaked. I bit down, holding my breath, when suddenly the door before me swung open, two hands grasped my plaid. Unceremoniously I was yanked inward to land with a crash on the planks at the Templar's feet. His sword was drawn and rested point down on my chest before I knew what had happened.

"What have ye heard? Who sent ye?" It was Seamus directing the interrogation.

"Nothing," I stammered, but it was an obvious lie.

"Come, Tormod, answer the question." The Templar's voice was calm. He didn't seem to be as alarmed to see me as did Seamus.

"I mean, my Lord Knight, I did hear ye, but it didn't make much sense. No one has sent me, save the Abbot. I don't know anything o' intrigue," I sputtered, shaking with the certainty that I was about to be killed.

The Templar removed the point of the sword and resheathed it. Then reaching down, he offered his hand to pull me to my feet. "I had hopes that ye would not be much drawn into the schemes of our making, but as I expected, fate has deemed otherwise."

I picked up the dagger that had fallen in the scuffle and moved to a large table covered with maps and instruments of sea travel. As casually as I could, I laid it there.

"Take it. Ye will need it someday," the Templar said.

Mine, I thought with awe. I picked it up quickly and slid it into my sporran before he changed his mind.

The Templar didn't continue the conversation nor did he speak more of what I'd heard.

"Where are we a' for manpower?" he asked.

Seamus replied, "The captain an' first mate were killed. All o' our crew remain."

"I can plot our course. We will alternate sailing the vessel," said the Templar.

"We must redivide the work load. Douglas's absence leaves us with a hole." Seamus said the last with a glare at me that set my face to burning.

Douglas, the old man whom in my recklessness I had killed. "I will take his place," I said, miserable and desperate to atone.

"You will never be half the man he was, rat," said Seamus.

The Templar motioned sharply at him. "Enough o' that."

Seamus had the grace to look chastised. "Fine, let him do the work, be our servant."

His servant! I spoke solely to the Templar. "I will do whatever ye need me to do. I can take the wheel as well.

I have done so for my da many times. Though this is a much larger ship an' I'd need some counsel at first."

"We'd be better off slitting his throat an' tossing him over the side," said Seamus. "He could be a spy."

"I'm not a spy!" I protested.

"No, ye're probably not. Ye stink a' it too badly to have stayed alive this long if ye were." With that he left.

I watched him go with relief. "He likes me little," I said, "an' I him less." I turned to the Templar, imploring. "I'm not a spy. I'm sorry. I didn't mean to listen."

"I think there are a lot o' things ye don't mean to do, Tormod, but ye do them nevertheless. Start thinking ahead. This is not a fireside tale. We are hunted. The price on our heads is redeemable whether we are alive or dead. One misstep by any of us, an' this will end. None of us can afford for this to end badly." He turned away.

This was more than I had heard him say in all the time that I had known him. It was a lot to take in. "I am sorry," I said meekly. "For everything. For falling an' alerting the enemy o' our presence. For causing the death o' Douglas . . ."

"Ye didn't —" he started.

I cut him off. "Aye. I did. An' I apologize for that. I didn't do it on purpose, but I take responsibility for the action."

He dipped his head in acknowledgment.

"But I'm not sorry I followed ye an' came aboard," I said doggedly. "I think that I was supposed to be there in that place at that time. I don't know why, but I'm sure o' it."

The speech was a bit self-important, but I was still stinging from his words. I looked down at my feet unable to face him and another remark I would not like.

"Aye. Ye're right. Ye're supposed to be here."

Whatever else he might have said, I did not hear for a strange chill riffled the air. His words reverberated within my head. I swayed with dizziness. Blood spilled over a cross. Red leaching onto a field of white. Metal on metal rang in my ears. Firelight danced on dark walls.

"Focus. Ground. Shield." Strange commands from the Templar pressed into my mind. I didn't know what he meant or what he wanted, and the vision continued to pound away at my mind.

Then suddenly it was as if a stiff breeze blew through my mind and I felt the vision slide slowly away. All at once I was back in the here and now.

The Templar was close before me, his face furrowed with lines of concern. I had not even known of his approach. "Hush ye now. It's gone," he said.

I stared at him long and hard, trying to reconcile the vision. I felt faint. My hands were fists of white gripping his vestment.

"Do the visions come to ye often?" he asked, sounding so earnest that I responded without thought. "Not very, but even that is more often than I'd like." My body shook. Twice now the visions had come to me in the presence of another. This strange seeing that had been with me from birth was changing somehow.

"Aye. The visions can seem a curse," he murmured. "Or a blessing. 'Tis all in what ye make o' it, Tormod. Tell me, why is it ye have no training in the basics of grounding?" he asked.

I had no idea what he was talking about. I had only shared a vision once, and I had great cause to wish I hadn't. Panic rose within me as my mind careened back to the memory I longed to forget. *The boat was capsized in the water. The father o' Torquil's friend Cormack floated facedown.* I had told Torquil of the vision and he told his friend. When the body was found, the whole of the village branded me a warlock. Torquil and I were never again as we once were.

I pushed it away, nearly forgetting in whose presence I now stood.

"What did ye see?"

I swore I would never again voice anything I had seen, but the Templar asked so plainly I was bound to answer. "I saw a broadsword waver, then blood on a cross." I didn't want to go on but felt I must. "I think I saw ye," I whispered.

He stopped me with an outstretched hand, his eyes commanding obedience. " 'Tis not a tale to be shared."

"But ye don't know," I said, frustrated. "I feel ye must take heed. What I see *happens*." I needed him to believe me.

He pulled away and moved off several paces. "Aye. But what ye see is not the whole an' not always the truth o' the future." He didn't make a bit of sense and my face must have shown it.

"Think o' waters running swiftly in a stream. Drop a pebble an' ye change the path but a little. Drop a boulder an' ye have a diversion. 'Tis the same with lives an' futures. What ye saw may happen, but what I do between now an' then could very well change the outcome."

He reached down and picked up a large black cat that had wandered in and began scratching its neck and ears. The animal purred loudly and with much contentment. "I also think 'tis a very bad thing to know yer own future," he continued. " 'Tis enough that I've heard what I have. I wish to speak o' it no more."

"You know o' the visions?" I said. "Do ye have them as well? I've never known another who does."

"Aye. I have the vision." He would have said more, but just then Brother Andrus came into the room. A sharp look from the Templar warned me to heed my tongue. I did, but inside I wanted to chase the monk away. I badly wanted to speak with the Templar. I was troubled. The visions had been coming to me for as long as I could remember. And in the whole of that time, each and every vision had come to pass just as they had been shown to me. Anxiously I moved around the central table, picking things up and putting them down again.

TEACHER

"Good morn to ye, Andrus." The Templar allowed the cat to jump from his arms then resumed his work with the charts.

"Good morn, Alexander. A strapping day. The air is clean and pure. It stimulates the soul." As I knew our conversation of earlier was not about to continue, I turned my attention to the newcomer.

"How is it that ye're different?" I asked the Templar. "The Brothers, as opposed to the Templars?" They seemed alike and yet not quite so.

"Andrus is a Cistercian monk. Our beliefs, as Templars, an' our religious practices are derived from theirs. The Templars are, however, a knightly version o' their order, the soldiers o' Christ. Both orders are sworn to poverty, chastity, an' obedience," the Templar said.

"Chastity?" It was not a word I knew.

"Aye. We are not allowed to marry or keep the company o' women."

All women, I wondered? It was not something I'd given thought to. Lasses, so far as I could see, were naught but an ache to the head anyway, but what about his mam? I didn't ask as he had continued.

"The Templar Order has a very specific set o' rules an' ordinances that are ours alone. But they are not to be shared with the uninitiated. Know only that we are a military order trained in all aspects o' warfare."

Now he was getting to it, I thought. "So ye use swords, bows, an' knives," I said. "An' train to joust an' fight mounted?"

"Aye. All of those things, but 'tis no' for tournament that we train. 'Tis to protect God's people."

"Aye. Ye defend those who choose to make the pilgrimage from the bandits on the roads." I knew that much from my cousin. "But ye do get to fight," I said, stabbing forward with an imaginary sword. Suddenly I remembered his daggers as they landed in the man's chest and brow. My gut heaved.

"Aye, we fight, but we give praise to God in equal

measure. We share many of the abbeys o' the Cistercian Brothers an' in return see to their safety."

Brother Andrus nodded and helped himself to a bannock. "It suits both, ye see."

The Templar continued. "Together we study mathematics an' astronomy, which is the patterns o' the stars an' sky. We map an' navigate the sea an' land." He gestured to the table. "These maps an' charts represent two hundred years o' travel."

I approached, interested. Da did all of the plotting, but it was to places he'd been scores of times. "Here is the first place we must travel." He pointed to a large mass of land on the map before him. "The land o' the Saxons. Ye've not been much beyond the villages?"

I shook my head no.

"Ye're far beyond your boundaries now," he said.

"How long did I sleep? How far have we traveled?" I asked, excited by the prospect of what I saw before me.

"It matters not. We've many days ahead. Ye've missed nothing."

From the moment we'd met, he had been serious and vigilant. Now, as I looked up to see him deep in a series of mathematical computations, he seemed at ease. He took pleasure from the work of divining our direction. That much was obvious.

"What o' the crew?" I asked. "Seamus said the captain an' first mate were killed. Do ye have enough men to operate a vessel as large as this?" The ship to me was enormous. It would take a crew of fifteen or more to see to the daily duties of sailing her.

"Aye. We lost two," he replied. "But we will make do."

I was quiet then, thinking of the faceless crew. I would know them, sooner or later. As the Templar said, we had a long distance yet to travel. I thought then of the trip, of being away from my home and my family. I'd wanted to get away for so long, but now that I had, I suddenly felt small and frightened. My fingers closed over the hourglass on the table. Its sleek shape seemed molded to my palm.

" 'Twas not long ago that the only way to gauge sea travel was by the glass in yer hand," the Templar said.

"Aye? I know naught o' gauging distances."

"I will take my leave now," said Brother Andrus with a smile, scooping up a bit of herring on the way. "When Brother Alexander has an eager ear, long lessons inevitably follow."

The Templar didn't acknowledge his remark. "The instruments that ye see here are o' a new breed o' navigation, Tormod. An' this—he hefted the object aloft—is the greatest o' all. 'Tis called an astrolabe."

It was beautiful in a way I was unaccustomed to. "'Tis old," I said, running my fingers along the timeworn brass.

"Aye. The Arabs have been using them for many years. This was a gift from a friend."

An Arab friend. I didn't know any Arabs or anyone who knew any for that matter.

He held the astrolabe by the small loop at its top. The strange instrument was a series of discs held through the center with a peg. The top layer was cut away and I could see the disks below.

"What do ye use it for?" I asked, lifting it. I turned it in the light spilling in from the window. It made strange patterns on the floor.

"Astrolabes can show us how the sky looks at a specific place an' a given time. If ye know where ye are, an' where ye want to go, then figuring out how long it might take to get there is simple."

The ideas he so easily proclaimed were enough to draw me readily into the discussion. We spent much of the morning at it. We spent much of the day at it.

I didn't hesitate in the asking of the many questions that came to mind. I sensed in him the mind of a teacher, one who would welcome the chance to share the knowledge he had accumulated. His passion for sea travel was strong. I took all he offered, absorbing everything I could.

A NEW BEGINNING

We met on deck at midday. The ship was moving along at a brisk clip. The winds were high and the weather was cool. Seamus was working the sail.

"Seamus. Take the wheel."

They switched positions. "Ye need to grasp the rudiments of sword work in battle," he said, advancing on me as if we had been in the middle of a conversation. "I'm sure ye know what 'tis like in theory, but let's see how ye'd fare in reality." He effortlessly flipped a sword to me on the outstretched blade of his own. It lifted off the deck like it was sailing on the wind. With no other choice, I reached out to catch it. Immediately my arms were dragged directly down to the deck and I tilted precariously. "Hah." His laugh was full of mirth.

"Right. We'll use something a bit lighter." He pulled a wooden practice blade and targe from the pile of equipment he'd had me bring up from the lower deck. I'd assumed it was for Seamus and himself. I was so very excited knowing now that it was for me.

"First then, stand straight, right foot advanced an' keep the center of yer body over yer left foot. Use yer shield for balance an' yer sword for defense." He stood behind me and fired off a rapid number of commands. I struggled to grasp them.

"We'll use this time to yer advantage, Tormod. As an idle mind is the devil's playground, sloth is an insult to God." With little warning he came at me. "Lift yer sword," he shouted, bearing down. I did, and my blade met his. The resounding crack echoed through my bones. "As I come from yer left, swing yer shield up an' take the blow. Aye. Get yer body beneath it an' solid up your legs."

Thwack. This time I felt it all the way down my backbone. I heard Seamus laugh and turned to see several of the crew had joined us on deck.

"Bring up yer sword to balance yer body as if it was swinging to and fro." I turned as he bid, and the flat of my practice blade met his. Instantly it skittered out of my hand, leaving my fingers stinging.

"Good. Still, ye have to keep ahold o' it." His words were encouraging, though his blows had little mercy. Again and again he had at me. For my part I stood and countered, working the various drills as well as I might. But it was far from the simple task it seemed. I had a great deal to learn. "We've got to work those muscles. Ye'll not have sword arms in a day, but this is the day to get them on their way."

Near on a candle mark later I collapsed onto the deck, winded, sweating, and aching in every part of my body. The Templar handed me a tankard of water. He was not even winded. "Enough?" he asked.

I hated to admit it. "Aye."

He clapped me on the shoulder. "Ye've done well for yer first day." Then turning, he called, "Seamus. Yer turn."

I struggled to make my burning muscles respond. I was sore from head to toe with welts in more places than I cared to admit, but I could hardly wait to see Seamus take his share of the beating, so I hurried.

"Watch an' learn," Seamus said as he moved away.

I made a mocking face behind his back and took the wheel.

The Templar and Seamus continued where I'd left off, but used real swords and shields. The onlookers who had watched me with interest but little comment swiftly came alive. Much as it bothered me, I had to admit that Seamus was good. His movements were smooth, unlike my jerking scramble to cover my tail hodgepodge. The Templar had moved from mentor to aggressor in moments. Together he and Seamus moved in a lethal, beautiful dance. The clash and slide of blade on blade, the clink of the flat, edge, and tip of the swords each had a different tone and volume. As

I watched them dodge and turn, spin to avoid confrontation, and add strength and power when there would be a direct hit, I was amazed. Would I one day fight that way?

As my body cooled and theirs grew more overheated, I became aware of an odd difference in the normal thrum of the world around me. The accelerated beat of their hearts, the feel of their blood pounded inside my head. I could almost read each of their moves and intentions at the same moment they had them. The sun came from behind a cloud, glinting on the Templar's sword, catching me straight in the eyes. I flinched and turned away, but the light followed.

The flame of a candle lit the space behind my closed eyes. The fragile edge of a parchment glowed and a word appeared where none had been.

Sound rushed back into my ears, and I had to grip the wheel to keep from falling. My tunic was soaked clear through, though it hadn't been quite that way when I'd finished sparring.

The Templar and Seamus had taken a break. Andrus appeared at my side with water. "Are ye well, Tormod?"

He urged me to drink as the Templar approached.

"Prayers begin shortly, Tormod. I suggest ye hurry or ye'll not have time to change."

My legs wobbled and I could barely lift my arms. *Prayers, again.* We'd done them twice already this morning. It was fair worse than Sunday at the kirk. But he hadn't asked me to join them. He expected it.

✠

The kneeling was the worst, especially with a sore body. My lips spoke the words that I had known since near on birth, but my mind was far away. The more I thought of the recent vision, the more I was convinced the edge of the map I'd seen was the map I had carried, the map that had been taken from me at the abbey. But in the candle's flame a word appeared where none had been before. I had the exact shape of it strongly in my mind.

"Tormod." The Templar's voice cut into my musing and I realized that I had stopped reciting my prayer. I looked over sheepishly and, at his scowl, continued. It seemed like days before we finished. My knees were trembling as I struggled to stand.

"Come with me," the Templar said.

What did I do now? I followed him anxiously to the forecastle. He said nothing until we were alone. "We have to do something about the visions ye're having."

I'd not expected this topic.

"Ye had another at the wheel." I was amazed that he would recognize this.

"Aye," I said. "I saw the map."

"Was that all?" He took up an ewer from the sideboard, poured out some water, and offered me some. I took it gratefully and dropped to a stool by the table.

"I saw a flame that was held beneath the parchment an' a word was illuminated. I canno' tell ye what it was, for I know not how to decipher letters well, but I know the shape of it." I took up a quill and dipped it into the inkpot near by. "Can I?" I asked motioning to a bit of parchment he had been scratching on.

"Aye. Go on," he said.

I took my time, but drew the shape that I knew to be letters. He watched avidly. "July is what it means." He looked at me oddly then, his mind working behind his eyes. "Ye told me that ye could no' read, an' the Abbot said that the soldiers took the parchment from ye. How is it that ye remember a map that ye didn't see?"

I assured him quickly. "I canno' read, but on the way to the preceptory I dropped the scroll an' the map fell out."

He didn't say more on the matter, but I could tell that I wasn't entirely free of this subject. "We'll have to do something about this lack o' reading ability as well. Our journey will be a long one. There's no reason we shouldn't put the time to use."

Lovely, I thought, *prayer and schooling. Was this what I'd escaped for?*

"First we have to work on something that ye're in dire need o', some safeguards against the visions."

I was intrigued. I didn't know much about the visions except that they came to me and they always happened as I saw them. He pulled another stool over beside mine.

"Each use o' the power changes us in some way," he began. "If ye recall, ye're often physically weakened immediately after ye have a vision, an' sometimes ye have a difficult time pulling yerself away an' back."

"Aye." I had noticed the very same, but I didn't know there was anything to be done about it.

"I want ye to work on what I show ye now every day, three times each day. It has to come to ye automatically. There is so much more to the power than just visions. We will take it slowly, but in this I will no' tolerate slacking."

I was put off by that remark but hid the way it stung. I'd just have to show him that I was serious. The whole idea of there being more than the visions set my skin tingling. "What do I have to do?" I asked.

"Ye must learn three commands: focus, ground, an' shield. I will take ye through them one at a time, an' we will practice." He sat up tall and stared deeply into my eyes.

"The focus is here." It was suddenly as if my mind

cleared. Like all outside thoughts were stripped away. "Nothing but the task at hand, like a hawk diving down on its prey, I want ye to empty yer mind of all but the vision itself. Ye will notice small details ye would no' otherwise have taken in."

I recognized what he did, but I had no idea how to do it myself. "Give it time. Ye will see how."

I felt as if he had read my mind. It was a bit unnerving.

"Ground is this." All at once the power of the land around me swirled through my mind. The wind rushed. I felt it on my skin and heard the roar of it in my ears. The earth thrummed. It was as if the ground beneath the deck, deep beneath the waves, reverberated. "Let it roll around ye, Tormod."

I could do nothing but let it do as it would.

"Now see it. Feel it. Let it fill ye from yer head to yer toes." I didn't understand, but he nudged something and a rush of color and sound flowed up from my feet and straight out through the top of my head.

"Now shield," he said. "Push all the power out o' yer mind an' body an' let it settle a' the very edges o' yer skin from the inside out." He didn't exactly do it for me but helped. I reeled at the odd twisting-tugging going on inside me. Then there was peace.

81

"That's it, Tormod. Ye did well this first time. Ye're on watch in a quarter candle mark. Why don't ye get something to eat an' think on what I've shown ye."

He stood and left me staring off to the distance.

✠

It was late and I was finding it hard to sleep. Around me the crew slept. The smells and sounds they made brought the blackness alive. I had always been a bit of a coward about the dark. At home, I slept near the hearth where the fire always glowed.

Home was truly far away now. I was on a ship with strangers, journeying to a place I didn't know. The missing came on me fast, and I found my throat tight.

I thought of Mam and Da, wondering how they fared and if they had by now heard I had gone. And then each and every one of my brothers' and sisters' faces ran through my mind, and I had the quick realization that I might never see them again. It was as if the mere thought would break my heart in two. I pulled the coverlet up to my ears and burrowed down, feeling the tears well. Then, from out of the darkness came a sound. Soft and low, the purr was completely welcome.

"Here, Cassiopeia," I called, dropping my hand down toward the floor. I could not see her but felt the presence of the cat moments before a tiny tongue scratchily lapped my fingers. She leapt to my chest, and I curled my fingers in the soft fur of her neck. Sleep came a short while later.

⁜

I marked the wall next to my hammock with a scraper Seamus gave me to clear the cracks in the decking. Fifteen days at sea. It seemed longer.

There was a strange sameness to life on the ship. We rose early and did our assigned duties; we prayed constantly and trained nonstop. I received lessons in reading, writing, and astronomy, and I learned to focus, ground, and shield.

Odd. I had thought that getting away would mean that I'd never have to do things that people demanded of me again. I was wrong.

If it was not the Templar, which I didn't mind at all, it was Seamus, heaping every horrible task aboard on my back. I looked at my hands. They were callused and cracked, and my legs were killing me.

Still worse, I was having trouble sleeping. My duties on watch tonight meant I had to rest during the daylight. I'd not gotten used to it.

"Tormod, I told ye to help even out the ballast before ye bedded down. O' course ye didn't." Seamus's voice cut across the dim quiet of the hold. "Get to it. Ye've duties to attend."

I gritted my teeth and swung my feet to the deck. Seamus was an unending source of misery. No matter what I did, it was not good enough. No matter how I tried, it was not what he would have. He harassed me nonstop.

"Move it, Tormod."

I wanted to beat the man bloody. I swear it. Every day during my prayers I asked God to strike him repeatedly with all of the plagues. But to no avail. I was not going to get the sleep I needed. Grumbling, I heaved to my feet.

From the stairs I heard coughing. One burst followed by another, and then a hacking wad of spittle was heaved somewhere off to my left. Seamus cleared his throat and sent one last parting jab. "Ye'll have to take the wheel this afternoon. I'll take the night."

I crossed the dark hold, pleased. Perhaps God had heard me after all. Seamus was ill. I hoped that he was miserable.

As I came up from below, I saw one of the deckhands, Horace, at work. The sweat gleamed on his dark-skinned back, and his arms, the size of great tree trunks, flexed beneath their burden.

It was Horace's job to shift the enormous rocks we

used as ballast to keep the ship evenly weighted. The constant crash of the waves undid his work nearly as fast as he'd accomplished it.

The duty was, to my mind, terrible. The stuff had a stink about it that was most unnatural. He said the rocks had been dredged from the harbor where the privy pits emptied. Still, even with that, he was of a good temperament. When I'd asked how he could be content doing what he did, Horace had told me that it took him up from the depths of the dark hold and into the light of day.

I understood not wanting to be in the dark, but not how he could find peace and contentment redoing the same job day in and day out. He actually sang as he worked, songs I'd never heard the like of before.

"Greetings, Horace," I called as I approached. It was good to give warning, else the strong man might heft a rock in your direction. He looked up and smiled, his teeth bright in the dark of his face. The smile was always a surprise to me. He was quite fearsome without it.

"A beautiful day, is it not, Tormod?"

I looked up to the cold, chill sky. "If ye say 'tis, Horace. I've come to help."

"I'm near on done," he said. "Don't trouble yerself."

Geordie, another of the deckhands, called out, "I could use ye here, Tormod, if ye're free. This damn mist is making the tar unpredictable. 'Tis thickening before I can apply it."

I hurried to his side and took the tar bucket and began to stir the mixture. Geordie was a small, wiry man whose duty it was to tar and retar, caulk and recaulk the planks all over the ship. This ensured that the wood remained strong and the seawater stayed out.

"What say, Geordie? D'ye think we'll be seeing the sun again this season?"

Geordie was bent low, and I dropped to the deck beside him. He dipped his brush and expertly sealed the space between the boards. "I don't know as we'll ever see her again, lad. My bones are surely not liking this cold damp."

Across the deck, the Templar stood at the wheel. "We'll be making land before nightfall, Tormod. I've sent Seamus to his pallet. Ye will accompany me."

I couldn't believe my ears. He was taking me ashore and leaving Seamus behind.

The afternoon passed like the slow drip of Geordie's tar. Excitement bubbled within me, but I was fearful as well. I recalled the conversation between the Templar and Seamus when first we'd boarded. We were going to the Archbishop to tell him the map had been taken. The thought nearly made me ill, especially as I was responsible.

LAND HO!

The Templar was correct in his calculations. The day was gray. A fine mist painted the decking where I huddled, watching and waiting. Finally the call came.

"Land ho!" the Templar shouted. "Tormod, ring the bell."

I scrambled to my feet and tugged strongly on the bell we used to announce the candle marks of the day. Deckhands came quickly from below.

"Oars, hard to starboard," the Templar shouted.

The ocean was wild and unsettled. As we closed the distance to shore, the ship rocked, fighting the direction of the crew's oars. I felt the Templar behind me at the rail, watching the ominous darkness crest beneath the waves. The rocks were still far below the surface, but they bore watching. It would be awful to come all this way and tear open the hull on a jut of rock.

The Templar took the wheel and fought to keep us on course. The two-ton wooden ship bucked and lunged, riding each wave and crashing through the trough with such force I had to grip the rail to keep from being thrown across the slippery deck. At first it didn't appear as if we were making any headway, but then, gradually, we began to turn and inch our way past the rough water and rocks into the calmer surf of an inlet.

My first view of English soil was a bit disappointing. The beach looked much like the one I'd left, and the trees and land far too similar to be such a vast distance as we had traveled from my home.

There was a great deal to be done and I, as much as anyone aboard, was eager to set my feet once again on solid land. I was coiling the rope to the sail when the Templar called over to me. "Go below and get ready to leave."

The loud clang of the iron links rumbling across the winch made the deck tremble as I crossed it.

✠

Within a candle mark we were ready to disembark. The mist had turned to a steady rain. I huddled within my plaid as a coracle was lowered down to the water. The Templar came up behind me. "Come. 'Tis time."

I feared this opportunity would never come. The rope ladder on the side of the ship was an easy feat. I was first into the boat, steadying myself as it rocked, and dropped quickly to sit. The Templar followed. We each took an oar and began to pull toward the rocky shore.

The wind picked up as we fought the waves, blowing spray into my face and down my neck. I ducked deeper into my plaid, pulling hard on the oars.

The boat was shallow and we were able to row in close. "I'll go first an' drag ye to the beach, so ye can jump to the sand." He bared his feet and rolled up his breeks to the knee. "No point in the both o' us freezing."

I was grateful. I was cold just being on the water. In the water would not be good at all. I grabbed his boots when the boat's hide scraped the sandy bottom and jumped ashore.

We dragged the boat up into the shadows of a copse of trees, and the Templar shrugged into his boots. A thin, curving track snaked through the dense woods. The rain dripped from the branches onto my head. I huddled waiting, wondering what lay ahead. And then we were off.

Beyond the trees, the visual similarity to home disappeared. A long, wide road stretched ahead, tamped solidly by those who had traveled and continued to traipse along its length. It was muddy and pocked with rain-filled ruts. I avoided them as best I could, but my boots were soaked in moments.

The town was surrounded by an enormous stone wall and appeared to have grown upward in a spiral toward the crest of a hill. Approaching the gates, I was stunned by its bulk. The wall seemed as tall as a mountain. "I've never seen anything like this," I said.

The Templar laughed, clapping me on the shoulder. "Aye. 'Tis awe-inspiring, but no more than the manor within. Let us not tarry. A warm room an' hot food await."

He shoved forward and I stumbled along staring gap-jawed. How such a feat as building it could have been accomplished, I could not imagine. It stretched above our heads and to our left and right beyond sight.

"The wall surrounds the whole o' the city," he said, nearly reading my thoughts. "There are towers built at regular intervals all around. An' there—he pointed upward—are walkways between that guards patrol. Look up as we enter."

I did as he suggested, though the rain drizzled in my eyes and down my chest. Amazed, I let out a hissing breath. A fearsome iron-studded gate hung suspended above our heads. If it were suddenly let loose, we would be skewered and crushed by the sharpened points of its base.

" 'Tis called a portcullis. 'Tis lowered at night or in case o' emergency when the city needs to be sealed off. There are two with a small passage between. Beyond the first ye'll see holes in the roof beams above. If an enemy makes it through the first gate, the second is dropped, an' hot oil or pitch is poured from above."

I shivered at the horrific image and moved quickly inside. The noise and smell hit me immediately, and a wave of travelers entering behind threatened to bring me to ground. Jostled and elbowed, I lost sight of the Templar. In a panic I spun around. A hand clamped my arm, and I was jerked roughly aside as a group who had come in behind us nearly plowed me down. "Stay with me, Tormod."

I didn't have a chance to argue as he tugged me along. A variety of shops lined the road's edge, and an open market was being held against one length of the great wall. We hurried through the rain, dodging the crowds that did business no matter the weather. I tried to absorb everything at a glance as I trailed. Merchants, with tarps staked and strung in a succession of low-hanging shelters, had arrayed their wares on wooden tables against the wall. There were vendors of fish and vegetables, booths of earthenware, jewelry, and weapons. Voices were raised in barter as customer and vendor argued over the best price. Bairns in wet homespun ran and played amid the booths as business went on around them. It was familiar to our trips to market. Chaos reigned, and yet it was life as usual for those involved.

"This way," he said, taking off along a road that snaked between two rows of shuttered houses. "Stay close and keep pace. We've a walk ahead to the manor and some o' these roads attract a rough sort o' traveler."

The smell in the alley made my throat close tight. I had often complained about the air belowdecks. Though open to the morning sky, this smelled worse, if that could be believed. Urine and refuse mingled beneath the onslaught of the rain and wafted up my nose, lingering in the folds of my plaid, which I held to my face. The Templar paid little attention to me as we walked, save to occasionally make sure I was still at his side. He seemed to withdraw deeply into himself, a condition I was getting to know fairly well. I didn't distract him with idle chatter.

I had no need, for I was engrossed in the new sights spread before and behind us. We traveled in a strange twisting that seemed to wind ever upward. I marveled that the Templar made his way unerringly, for there were a good many turns we took that I would have thought would wind back on themselves and end our journey. He had obviously been here before.

Below us the town spread like a tapestry woven with dark, vivid colors and sharp blackness. The higher we climbed, the more enthralled I became. The manor was on the very tip of the rise, and I craned my neck to see past the sheer walls of rock that surrounded it. When finally the road we traveled ended, we stood before a formidable gateway. There were two dark wooden doors at least six arm spans wide, crossed by bands of hammered iron.

The Templar used the hilt of his sword to gain attention from within. I felt the thump of his rap in my chest. Far above our heads on the stone walls a guard appeared. The Templar spoke. "I am Alexander Sinclair, Knight o' the Holy Temple o' Solomon. I was told Archbishop Lambert is within. I wish an audience."

AUDIENCE WITH AN ARCHBISHOP

My knees felt suddenly too weak to hold me upright. An Archbishop . . . the rank to me was as would have been the King. Though I knew this was the man who the Templar sought, it didn't hit me until this very moment that I might be in his company when it happened. The child of a fisherman in the presence of one most holy . . .

"Our great Lord was a fisherman, Tormod," the Templar said with amusement.

I shook my head in disbelief: again this reading of my thoughts. He had done it several times now, and it was unnerving.

He smiled. "Ye mumbled, Tormod. As ye do more often than even ye can recall."

It was a long wait. We huddled beneath the small overhang of the wall, avoiding the worst of the downpour. My plaid enveloped the whole of me, but I was far from warm. It had rained so much that the wet now penetrated the heavy wool, and I was chilled from the bones out. At times it crossed my mind that we might be turned away. The Templar kept his hand resting lightly on the haft of his sword, his body set in a rigid stance between the door and myself. Thoughts again pummeled my mind. *Could we be walking into an ambush?* Just then the great doors swung slowly inward. And my heart sank.

The doors didn't open to the main residence but to another winding, now cobbled, road. I suppressed a groan. Whatever was to come, I wished that it would finally come to pass, for I'd have given my right arm for a warm fire and a space out of the rain. We passed through a series of arches, outer buildings, and large open spaces. When finally we were shown to the grandest of them all, I realized we had reached the pinnacle of the heights. I stopped for the barest of moments and looked down, back from where we'd come.

Ours was the most wondrous of views. Below and all around us was a patchwork of color. At first glance I understood why I had been so drawn to the map. From my current height the whole of the land looked like one great parchment — as if the world had suddenly flattened. If I looked at any one particular area, I could quickly make out the individual rise and fall of the village in the distance. The trees were great billows of green and brown, and when I looked at the land as a whole, one thing blended into the next.

The Templar had already moved toward the manor, and I scrambled to keep from being left behind. All the while the image of the map, the one that haunted my memory from the first, stood sharply in my mind's eye.

The manor, as he called it, was no less than my idea of a castle — a great house of stone built into the rock of the hillside. It was several stories tall and stretched back and away so that I could not see where it actually ended. A servant dressed in robes of gray linen met us at the door and escorted us inside.

The entranceway was dark, and I craned my eyes to see in the dim space before me. The sconces on the walls held beeswax candles. They smelled pleasant but didn't throw off much light. The room, however, was a haven of warmth, and I reveled in the difference.

"I will take your outer garments and lay them by the fire," said the servant. "The Archbishop will see you momentarily. He is in conference. I will be back to escort you."

The Templar nodded and, as soon as the man was out of sight, moved furtively toward the entrance ahead, staying close to the wall as he peered beyond. I made a move to follow, but he forestalled me with an open hand. I moved instead to the wall closest. A group of paintings were set in frames on the walls — men in formal dress. I'd never seen images portrayed so realistically. *How incredible,* I thought, *to be able to capture a likeness that way.* I slid my fingers along a rounded cheek and across an ear and was surprised to find the surface rough and dry. My mind expected to feel the soft and wrinkled skin my eyes so clearly beheld.

"This way, Brother Knight. The Archbishop awaits you." The Templar started after the servant of the house, and I reluctantly left the paintings to follow. So dim was the corridor that I barely saw the men whose backs I followed. We were shown into an enormous room lit by a multitude of glowing, golden lights. Tapers, tallow candles, and the flames of lit straw rushes abounded, so much so that I had to blink several times to accustom myself to the brilliance.

The Archbishop was seated on a richly appointed chair facing the door through which we entered, and he rose as we were announced. He was large, with wide shoulders and a light olive complexion. His hair was white like his robes, a set of unornamented linen, and yet his bearing proclaimed his rank as a high official of the Church. I hung back, awed.

"Brother Alexander, God's hand has guided ye to me."

"Aye, it has, Yer Grace, an' we are humbled an' thankful o' it." He knelt before the Archbishop and kissed his ring. Then gaining his feet, he said, "I have troubling news nonetheless an' had hoped ye might counsel me in a few matters."

His gaze flicked to mine and back to the knight. "I am always yer servant, Alexander."

"My pardon, Yer Grace," said the Templar. "Allow me to introduce my apprentice, Tormod MacLeod. He is a rare lad an' will be a welcome addition to the Order." He turned to me. "Tormod, present yerself."

I nearly stumbled as I crossed the short space between us and sank to my knees to kiss the ring before me. *A Templar's apprentice? Could he possibly be serious?* I had dreamt half my life of the possibility. "Yer Grace." I spoke breathlessly. " 'Tis an honor."

He turned to the Templar. "I would speak to ye privately a moment, Alexander. Help yerself, Tormod. There is food set out beyond that door. Break yer fast. We will no' be long."

I was nearly as glad of the excuse to absent myself from the piercing gaze of the Archbishop as I was happy to indulge in food that was hot and not salted or dried. I moved quickly across the room and through the door to give them their privacy.

The chamber I entered was richly appointed. Heavy, vividly embroidered tapestries lined the walls, and in a great hearth real coal burned. I stretched my hands to the warmth. Peat, the turf we used in my homeland, never burned as hotly as this.

On a long table were dishes upon dishes, platters of stuffed eel and pheasant, sweet onions and plums, puddings of rich reds and browns, and breads drizzled in honey and coated with almonds. Even on the highest feast days the family had never such an assortment at one time. *A Templar's apprentice,* I thought. *Could it really be true?*

As I ate and my body warmed, I became aware of a need that had been pressing in on me for much of our trip up the hill — something I had forgotten in the presence of the Most Holy Archbishop and the prospect of food. I had to make water. And at this moment it was a desperate urge.

I fidgeted, willing my unhappy bladder to cease its pressure, but my body was in no mood to take yet another of my mind's commands. At last I knew I had to find the garderobe or I'd make a fool of myself.

⚜

I crept into the chamber, quietly so that I would not intrude on the Templar and His Grace's discussion. If I could but slip by unheeded, I thought, perhaps the servant beyond would give me direction.

But as I skirted the edge of the chamber, my eyes turned toward the two at the dais. The Templar was down on one knee with his head bent low. The Archbishop stood before him, and in his outstretched hands was a small carving. It was an odd scene, to be sure, but something even stranger happened then. On my skin I felt the waft of a warm breeze — a breeze with no origin in an enclosed room. I stopped, perplexed, my eyes riveted to the scene before me.

Suddenly the darkness of the carving began to slowly change. It grew brighter and the wind blew stronger. The candle flames flickered in a way that made the room shimmer with light.

Without thought I dropped to one knee mirroring the position of the Templar. In moments the whole of the chamber was as bright as the pure light of day. I heard the Archbishop's voice from far away. His words were in a language of beauty unknown to me.

The golden glow of the room seemed to crowd around me, blotting out the form of the men, and sound rose in my ears. "Blasphemer! Heretic!" I felt the crowd around me, angry, pressing me forward against a barrier.

Up above, a platform hovered and the smell of burning wood curled in the air.

"Focus. Ground. Shield." The Templar snapped the words at me and I felt myself react. The force of the vision broke, but my eyes and mind were still filled by the scene. My body trembled.

The Templar was on his knees before me. "Shhh, leanabh." The Gaelic endearment felt like home, but I was far away. "'Tis gone. Ye are safe. Breathe deeply."

"A crowd was gathered. They were frightened. Four men were brought in in chains."

My words came haltingly, but I forced my impressions into the air of the chamber. "High above, a man shouted, 'Blasphemer! Heretic!'"

The Archbishop stepped down from the dais. I felt his eyes on me, staring as if I were a specimen in an alchemist's lab. "What more did ye see?"

"I don't know," I said. "Nothing. 'Twas images an' sounds, colors an' feelings." I struggled to explain how the visions came to me. My breath felt short, my chest tight. My head was swimming.

The Archbishop approached. The Templar and I stood. "To see what lies ahead is a frightening ghost." He spoke softly, almost as if he were riddling something out for himself. I wondered why he was not surprised at my vision state.

"I cannot stay with ye for I must ready to journey to Rome. Stay. Eat. Warden de Kendall's staff will see to your reprovisioning." His mind was elsewhere, already dismissing our presence.

"A moment, Yer Grace, if I might . . ." Their eyes turned toward me. My face burned. My body's persistent need still compelled me and I felt a sudden embarrassment. "A chamber pot?"

"Are you ill?" The Archbishop moved quickly to the sideboard and drew a pot from beneath.

"No, but if I don't hurry, I will be wet."

My words were so completely out of place that the Templar let burst a sharp laugh. Shaking his head, he said, "Beyond the door is a garderobe, Tormod." The bewildered smile that played about his lips distracted me from the worries that lingered in my mind.

HISTORY LESSON

I met up with the Templar a short time later in the same room I had begun to feast in earlier. Two chairs and a table had been set while I was away. I dropped down opposite, feeling tired and worried. The vision made me uneasy.

The Archbishop had arranged with the castle's keeper for fresh supplies to be readied while we ate. Two large packs lay on the flags at the Templar's feet.

"Templar Alexander?" I asked.

"Hmm," he murmured, distracted.

"Is this the Archbishop's residence?"

"What?" he said, pulling back from the path his thoughts had taken.

"This castle. Is it all for the Archbishop?"

He looked down the table as if seeing it for the first time. "No. The Archbishop is here on business to Rome. He is friends with the Lord Chancellor of Dover and so stays here when he visits." He finished his last bite. "We should be on our way. Are ye done?"

I nodded. Though I was hungry and the food abundant, I ate little. I could not seem to push the vision from my mind.

At full dark we set out once again. It was still raining and the sky was a lead gray, which seemed fitting as that was the way I felt.

"Tormod, I don't need to tell ye that ye must not speak o' the carving with any aboard, aye?" he said after we passed through the first archway.

"Aye," I replied. "But we're not aboard yet. What is this thing?"

He looked as if he would put me off, but nodded, as if to himself. "Stop here."

The temperature had dropped while we were inside. It was cold and I was uncomfortable. On a stone bench in an alcove against a high hedge we sat. His face was grave when he turned to me.

"We have to be careful, Tormod, now more than ever. I know no' what yer vision portends, but the fact that it has come to ye with the aid o' the carving makes me leery. These particulars *are* quite probably destined to happen."

"Everything I *see* happens," I mumbled. He ignored my words. "The carving," I prompted. "What is it?"

He was silent a moment. "I will start a' the beginning. I'm not certain that it is good for ye to know so much, but I don't seem to have a choice in it. Many o' my visions have included ye."

I was not surprised, since I'd heard him speak of it to Seamus, but to hear it again said directly to me in so plain a manner made me feel a bit off. I wondered if his visions involved blood and injury. A shiver ran through me and I tucked my hands beneath my plaid to still their shaking.

"Do ye recall what I told ye o' the origins o' the Order?" he asked.

"Aye," I said, remembering. Hugues de Payen, a knight of France, had joined the Crusade to liberate

God's Kingdom in Jerusalem. He arrived with high ideals only to be shocked at how poorly trained and ill equipped the men who had flocked to the Church's cause truly were. Those who fought fell quickly beneath the Muslim swords. Those who roamed the roads were easy prey to the bands of mercenaries.

Hugues had called to him eight strong knights, related by blood and marriage, and approached the King with a proposition. If the King would back them, these men would dedicate themselves to patrolling the roads and giving what protection they could to the pilgrims. They started out, nine men based out of the palace stables, a place said to be located atop the ancient Temple of Solomon. They'd named themselves the Poor Fellow Soldiers of Christ, but the world came to know them as the Knights of the Temple of Solomon or, more simply, the Knights Templar.

"What have the origins to do with the carving?" I asked.

"Tormod, Hugues de Payen was gifted, as ye an' I are gifted," he said.

"He had the vision sense?" He had not shared this with me. I leaned foward, determined not to miss a word.

"Aye. An' while sleeping in the stables, turned into a dormitory, he saw a storehouse built into the bedrock o' the original temple. He an' his men excavated —"

"An' they found the carving!" I burst in.

"Aye. Along with a library o' scrolls an' a host of gold, treasure, an' jewels."

My mouth dropped. *Treasure.* I knew what I thought was the history of the Knights, but I had never heard of a store of ancient treasure. The night seemed to grow darker as he spoke, the rain and clouds growing thicker. I remained quiet as he continued, fearing if I broke the spell, he would stop.

"The carving we named Baphomet, meaning wisdom, for in its presence all o' our kind, the gifted, experience an enhanced vision sense."

His eyes were steady and a great rush of excitement overtook me.

"Why do ye have it now?" I asked, impatiently. "What has it to do with the Archbishop?"

"What ye overheard on the ship that first day is part o' this," he said. "The Templars, as ye know, are the right hand o' the Pope. We've been that from the beginning. We answer only to the Holy Father — no sovereign, no acolyte, no one — an' in return the Holy Father relies on us for things he would ask o' no other."

I squirmed on the bench, desperate to know more.

"Three an' a half years ago a map came into the hands o' Pope Boniface. It had been found in a cave a' the edge o' the sea, sealed in a jar o' clay. In the right-hand corner was a drawing, an exact image o' the carving

I hold here." His hand curved around his sporran where the bulk rounded out its shape.

"Tormod, Pope Boniface an' his successor, Pope Benedict, as well as a few select members o' the Church, are part o' a secret upper-echelon sect o' the Templar Order."

"They're Templars?" I asked, incredulous.

"Not in the ordinary way. They took no vows, but are a part o' a group who oversee the greatest decisions concerning the Order," he said.

A secret sect of the Templars, and he trusted me with the knowledge. I could scarcely credit it.

"Pope Boniface immediately recognized the image o' the carving from the map an' sent it to the Order in Paris. But things in France were getting a bit tense, an' it was judged prudent to move both map an' carving to Scotland."

"Why? What was happening?"

"Pope Boniface clashed with King Philippe an' excommunicated him. The King retaliated by having the Pope kidnapped."

I was horrified. That anyone should think to kidnap a Pope was beyond my wildest imagining.

"The Templars rescued Pope Boniface, much to the anger o' the King, but it was too late. He was old an' the experience harsh. He died a month later."

"And then?"

"Benedict was next in line for the Papacy, but he was no' long in power."

"Why?"

"Philippe's man poisoned him. Can ye credit it? I had a vision, not five paces from the King a' court, while I was picking up tribute owed the Order. I saw Guillaume de Nogaret, the King's councillor, take the Papal ring from the Pope's dead finger." He shook his head.

"I've never killed a man in cold blood," he said. "But in this instance, I think that I should have."

I nearly reeled at his words. "Ye could not. Ye would not. 'Tis no' the way o' the Templar."

He didn't move or blink. "He has killed two o' the most holy an' powerful men in the world. Let us hope my inaction has no consequences for the future. I left him free to continue his reign o' recklessness, Tormod. Was that something a Templar should have done?"

I was suddenly colder than at any other time. It was as if a frigid wind whipped across my soul.

"Somehow Philippe knows about the map. He's tracked us from Paris to Scotland."

"That's when ye found me," I said.

"Aye. I saw ye in a vision, carrying the map to the Abbot in my stead."

"Ye gave it to me," I said. "An' I gave it up to those hunting ye."

The Templar nodded. "But why would the carving

have me entrust the map to ye, if only it was to be lost," he said almost to himself.

"If yer visions are like mine, then what ye see is the future. The carving is not directing; it is just relaying what is to happen." I was nearly mumbling to myself trying to figure it out.

"Unless . . . I was meant to carry it, so that I could later redraw it for ye. I can, ye know! I know its lines an' shapes like I know my homeland."

"Maps are no' simple things, Tormod. They must be precise an' accurate," he said. " 'Tis a good thought, but ye only could have seen it for a moment, an' that's not enough to redraw it." He stood, dismissing my offer.

"Listen to me. I know the map like 'tis still here afore me. I have oddness with things that I see. I remember. Even if I see something for only a moment, it stays."

He stared at me, weighing the possibility. "We will try it then. Stranger things exist in this world than a good memory. Particularly when it comes to the carving."

"I can do it." I said with confidence, getting to my feet and shaking off the rain that beaded on my plaid.

"Where do we go from here?" I asked.

"To the Grand Master. I still have the carving an' I need to get it to a safehold."

The idea seemed preposterous. "Is he not in France, where the soldiers who are seeking ye reside?"

"He's due to tour the Spanish preceptories before going on to Paris. We will seek him there, in Spain. I have allies who will help. Remember what I have said an' do not speak o' this to any."

A SECRET HELD

The moment we boarded, the Templar installed me at the table in the forecastle. With several parchments, a quill, and ink, I got to work though it was not as easy as I had originally imagined. It was one thing to see a map, a whole other to draw it. I had some trouble with the scale and proportion, but the shape of things came to me easily.

Several marks of the candle later, I got it right. The last bit was the most difficult: the strange series of dots scattered across the surface. I fussed over these the most. When I'd added the last, my eyes drifted down over what I'd drawn. Something was not quite right, I thought, tracing the map. Suddenly the candle flickered in a draft from the window. The memory of the vision I had came back to me. *Julio.* I added the word in the lower left-hand corner.

The Templar came in as I was sanding the ink on the final bit. He stood beside me and I held my breath waiting.

"Well, from what I can recall it looks right." He stared at it thoughtfully. "Julio. . . . Thank ye, Tormod. I'll take it from here."

I stood and wriggled my fingers, pleased. He had already moved into place and forgotten me. I wandered out of the forecastle, back toward the ladder to the hold. Seamus blocked the way. "Geordie needs ye aft, move on."

"But I've been working for —" My protest was cut off by his look.

"Now."

Plagues, God. Boils and famine would work. A few dozen locusts down his back and in his breeks. Feel free to drop them now.

✠

The Templar worked closeted away for the next two days. Near noon on the third, I felt his shadow over me as I caulked the decking with Geordie.

"I need ye tonight, Tormod. We are going to shoot the moon. 'Tis time yer lessons resumed."

I squinted up at him. He seemed pensive, as if his mind were still far off in calculation. "Aye," I said.

"Geordie, can ye do without the lad? I'd like him to sleep a bit."

"Aye, Captain. 'Tis not as if the boards are goin' anywhere. Prevention, this is. Get ye gone, ye bilge rat." I smiled at Geordie's good-natured chafing. His names for me changed by the day.

"Ye need me an' ye know it, old man." I tossed a floppy straw hat to him. "Cover yer head before ye burn out what little mind ye've got."

The Templar cuffed me as I passed. "Respect for all, Tormod. A knight can be funny but not disrespectful o' an elder."

I ducked my head guiltily but caught Geordie's wink as I stowed my bucket. The Templar walked away.

"Bilge rat," Geordie said beneath his breath.

✠

The night sky was black and the stars winked like fireflies. Not a cloud marred the view, not a wind crossed the bow. I stood at the wheel as I had for the last several candle marks. Tonight's lesson was how to shoot the moon. I looked forward to it. The astrolabe, our charts, quills, and ink lay on a plank set across two casks. We were to take our headings from the height of the moon from the horizon as it related to the position of several stars.

The door to the forecastle creaked behind me, and in the still blackness I saw the silhouette of the Templar silently cross the deck.

"Have the others gone below?" His question was nearly lost in the wash of the sea, and suddenly, for no reason I could fathom, the skin on the nape of my neck prickled.

"Aye. None have been about for more than a candle mark." I matched my tone to his, not knowing why, but sure that it was something I should do. He stepped into the moon's shimmer of light and I saw that he carried a small bundle in his hands. He glanced quickly about and laid his burden on the plank beside our equipment.

Recognizing the wrappings, I stepped back, uncertain and no little bit frightened.

"Prop the wheel an' come to me. Be quick about it, the moon is even now reaching its apex."

I looked up. The moon seemed full, but I had no experience to judge the absolute peak of the cycle. "What must we do?" I asked.

He unwrapped the carving. This close I could see what I was not able to before. It was made of hardwood, stained dark with age. It was a woman. She was on her knees, but sitting back on her heels. Her hands were lifted above her head, palms up, as if reaching, waiting.

The Templar moved behind the cask and crouched, looking at the carving. He shifted it several times, and it took me a moment to realize he was arranging the figure according to his sight of the moon. When the form was where he wanted it, he said, "Hand me the astrolabe."

"What are we doing?" I whispered, giving it to him.

"Following a vision," he said mysteriously.

I watched as he turned the astrolabe's back to us and then placed the instrument into the hands of the carving. "God's toes," I gasped. It was a perfect fit, as if one had been made for the other.

The warm rush of air and the tingling of a million pinpricks that I had felt before in the carving's presence flowed across my skin as the carving began to glow. Its brilliance lit the ebony of the night with a cascade of shimmering stars. And as I looked on these, lights began to lessen and spread out, their tiny reflections winking on the dark wooden planks at my feet.

"Here, Tormod. Hurry. Crouch an' tell me what ye see."

I moved to his side and took a sighting through the center of the astrolabe. My breath caught tight in my throat. The brilliant sparkles of light that radiated from the carving were exactly in position with the myriad of stars surrounding the moon. As I stared and the moon reached its fullest, the lights began to flicker, growing stronger and brighter, filling the space in my mind, turning to dots. Black on a page, atop an etching that shifted from lines of ink to the sharp clear edges of a real mountain. Valleys dipped in the folds that formed before me. Water careened over a ledge, the crash of it filling my ears.

Focus. Ground. Shield. Abruptly, the world shifted and I swayed. The carving before me turned black once again.

"Are ye all right, lad?" His words came to me from far away, but his hand on my arm felt solid.

"I am well." I murmured, the vision still strong within me.

"What did ye see?"

"The stars mark the map. They're laid over it."

He smiled and nodded. "I had a suspicion," he said and crouched. I watched, waiting.

"Did ye have a vision?" I asked breathlessly.

"No," he said. "I see only stars."

"But why would ye have me look first? Why did it only work for me?"

"I don't know, but I dreamt last night o' ye doing just this," he said. "The carving is once again providing the key."

"Ye speak in riddles. The key to what?"

"Finding what's been left for us to find," he said.

"Back to the wheel, now. We'll have to shoot the moon another night."

✠

The Templar spent much of the next few days closeted away with his maps and charts. Whenever I stopped by the forecastle between shifts or just during the quiet of afternoon, he was elbow deep in mathematical formulas that he scratched on every available surface.

In midmorning of the fourth day, I was at loose ends. I had finished the Matins prayers and stood at the aft part of the ship with nothing to do. The weather was downright eerie, the sky a deep and forbidding gray. The rain and wind had died off during the night, but the air was still and cold. I huddled in my plaid by the rail staring at the ominous deep green of the ocean. Barely a ripple marred the surface, and the sail hung slack.

Seamus had the wheel. I watched him across the length of the deck. His face was pinched; something worried him. Unease slid through me. "Tormod, get Alexander."

He almost never addressed me directly without some kind of a venomous jab. So I was surprised. I shot him a sideways look, but did as he bid. I bolted to the forecastle and popped my head inside. "Seamus needs ye."

115

The Templar looked up. His eyes were tired, red-rimmed and bleary. "Aye." He laid aside the maps and quill and followed me outside, scanning the ship, sail, and sky as he moved. "What is it?" he asked Seamus.

I felt it then, or rather I didn't feel it and knew.

"There's no wind. Not a stirring since last night." His voice was grim. Wind didn't mean much to a fishing vessel, but on a ship this size, it was nearly essential to travel. The Templar moved to Seamus's side and took the wheel, peering anxiously ahead.

"We should be all right for a while. We have enough provisions. The barrels o' ale from the Archbishop, an' the food is plenteous."

For some reason I felt the Templar's words were not as confident as they might be. "How fare the water barrels?"

"Two o' the eight are contaminated," said Seamus. "We have enough for a normal journey, but I don't know."

A white sail billowed in the forefront of my mind. Wind whispered in my ears.

"It will be enough," I said, lurching back to the present.

"It will be enough," the Templar echoed, striding across the deck and back to his maps.

✠

116

Day passed into night, then again into day. Everyone took their turn at the oars, moving us slowly across the calm water. I was as jumpy as a kitten. It was my prophecy that the wind would come. Part of me knew it would — everything I saw *happened*. But it was not an easy wait.

Seamus was even more affected than I. The longer we were forced to slowly crawl our way across the expanse of blue, the edgier he became. He took to prowling the perimeter of the ship in unending sweeps, constantly eyeing the horizon. But nothing he did changed the course of our placid wake. The Templar watched for the wind's change with no less impatience, yet he at least appeared calmly accepting of the situation.

I was above deck, off in a shadowed corner, casting my net when Seamus's voice reached me.

"Alex, we canno' go on like this. We must alter our course an' go back the way we've come." His outburst was loud, even in my ears a challenge.

"Our course is Spain." The Templar's voice was low but his authority carried.

Seamus paced away and back, agitated. "I have a very bad feeling."

"I canno' heed ye this time, Seamus. Yer visions are not specific enough; the power comes to ye sketchily. It could mean anything. We must continue. We will lose too much time going back. Unless ye've seen something more specific than what we spoke o', we continue on."

Seamus paled, and a slight tremor wracked his body. "No. I've seen nothing more."

The Templar turned away, but I could see that he was bothered. "It will be all right, Seamus," he said, slowly pacing before the rail. His mind was working, puzzling out the bits and pieces he had already encountered.

Seamus swallowed hard. He looked my way and his usual animosity appeared, then he turned back to the bleak horizon. "This damn stillness is killing me," he said. "Mark my words, Alex, something bad is about to happen, an' if we go on, we are powerless to stop it."

The Templar did not turn back, but I knew from the sudden tension in his posture that the words had reached something inside him. The small hairs on my arms prickled as he turned his eyes to my darkened corner and, for no reason I could justify, I felt suddenly frightened.

"Things are changing. I can feel it." The knight's words were meant for me. "We go on as we are, windless or not, and put in to Santiago."

Seamus sighed with a depressed sort of acceptance. "As ye will it, Uncle."

WINDS OF CHANGE

By nightfall the ship was back under a steady breeze and tensions aboard began to turn as well. That is, everyone's mood improved but Seamus's. The man literally vibrated with anger, and it was all the worse when he was near me.

Reason or no, things between us remained balanced on the edge of a blade. While the others returned to their tasks, the Templar bade me continue to fish, ending for a time my duties with the deckhands. This appeared to chafe Seamus all the more. Truth be told, I would have caulked the entire hold or rowed for days rather than spend time on deck with that man, for fishing gave him even more opportunity to cause havoc in my world. Nothing pleased him. Not my skills, nor the catch, nor the way I handled the wheel. Not even my scrubbing of the privy was good enough for the sergeant. I dreaded his presence around me.

The pale gray dawn brought with it a tiding of things to change. The wind whipped briskly across the deck as I dropped the first of our nets, letting the line slowly drift out and down. It was heavy and slick in my hands. I felt the bite of it in my fingers and the weight of it in my arms. Balance was a fine line I trod. I tipped over the rail, and the blood rushed to my head as I slowly lowered the bulk of the net seaward, making sure it fell evenly and didn't tangle.

The water was rough, crashing against the hull and rushing up in a spray that wet my arms as I dangled. The waves surged and dropped away, surged and dropped away. On one deep dip of the ship, as I was letting out the last of the net, I was surprised by the feel of someone behind me. I twisted to see what was going on. I saw and felt him at the same time.

Seamus's fingers closed over my shin. I didn't stop to ask questions, but kicked out and caught him square in the chest. It all happened so fast. He staggered back and cursed. I saw the rope tangle and tried to right myself, but the sea tugged the net out of my fingers. Then Seamus was yanked over the side.

What possessed me then I'll never know, for in truth I hated the man, but the moment he went over I grabbed my fishing knife, tossed aside my plaid, and dove in.

The water hit me with a crush, nearly tearing the knife from my grip. It was colder than the first ice of winter, and though my eyes stung, I searched for him in the blackness. In moments my ears were ringing and the pressure in my chest grew unbearable. He was deep and struggling. The rope was wrapped tight and grew more tangled by the moment.

I swam toward him to try and loose the rope, but he fought me off. The burning need for air made my head pound, but I ignored it and made a lunge for him.

This time I got close enough, for by now Seamus had stopped struggling. With the breath heaving in my chest, I sawed until the rope frayed and broke. With Seamus limp in my arms, I kicked for my life.

The surface glistened above, taunting me. His heavy, awkward body shoved me deep each time I reached for it, struggling to get Seamus's face and my own above the waves. The undertow was strong, fighting to suck me below, churning water into my open, gasping mouth. My body was exhausted and not working as it should.

"Tormod!" The Templar's voice floated over the roar of the sea and hope grew where none had been. I swam in circles, looking and listening, but the waves were coming from all directions, confusing me. A great crest broke over me and the force of it wrenched Seamus from my grasp. I began to choke on water that rushed down my throat. My chest was exploding as I fought again for the surface, and when at last I broke through, I knew that I'd lost him.

STARLIGHT

I ducked beneath the waves again and again, stroking though the dark, desperate to find Seamus. The water was so cold I couldn't tell if my arms or legs were moving. Somehow the direction I thought was the surface never seemed to be right. Blackness was all around me. The only heat I felt was the burn in my chest. I thought I was going to die.

Suddenly the darkness broke, and a glow of brilliant light filled the ocean's depths. I swam as if in a dream. No — as if in a vision. Before my eyes a thousand embers glowed. One by one the lights winked off and on, calling me forward.

With the breath so tight in my chest, every heave turning me inside out, I followed the trail of starlight. And as I passed each glowing point, my need for air lessened and my body warmed.

An eternity later I broke through the waves, gasping for air, determined to float. I heard them then, the Templar foremost in the shouting, and long moments later, I was hauled aboard.

"Tormod, lad, come back."

The Templar's soft voice called to me through a haze of mist. I heard him, but I could not speak or seem to come fully awake.

I drifted and dreamt. Though I don't know how long I stayed in that strange and silent place, I knew full well the waking.

Pain seared into my dreaming and I jerked to. The chamber was dark and frightening. The black wrapped around me and squeezed the air from my body.

"Lay still, Tormod. I'll get Alexander. He wanted to be told the moment ye woke." Seamus's voice startled me.

My eyes darted around the room, frantic. Nothing looked familiar. "Where am I? What's wrong with me?"

"Ye're in my quarters. Be calm." He moved quickly toward the door but didn't pass through it right away. He stood instead as if he could not move on. Suddenly he pounded the wall. "Why? Why would ye do it? I gave ye no reason to play savior."

I struggled to remember, to understand his words. The feel of the icy water closed in on me. "The water. We were in the water," I said raggedly. "I could no' find ye." It was all so bleary in my mind. I remembered the dark and cold and shook with the thought of it.

He hunched by the door, brooding. "I would not have done it for ye." He seemed embarrassed by what he'd said, but it made little sense to my mind. I didn't reply. I could not. Fear choked the words in my throat. *It hurts. My leg . . . the burn.*

"If there was something I could do or undo, I would."

I struggled to sit, and the pain ripped through my body. I howled with it.

He moved quickly across the room. "No, lie down. Ye'll tear the stitches." He pushed me flat, and I'd not the energy again to rise. *Stitches.*

Seamus left me then, in the dark that seemed to smother me. It felt like a candle mark, though probably only moments passed before the Templar opened the door. A blur of fur streaked past him and leapt onto the pallet. My leg throbbed beneath the cat's weight. "Cass, get off him," he said, shooing the animal away. Cassiopeia jumped from the bedding but stayed at my pallet's side. I could hear her purr in the darkness. It was comforting, and yet I squeezed my eyes shut. I wished to never open them and know the truth I would hear. "Tormod, I am truly glad that ye've finally awakened."

"What's happened? I know there's something. Something bad."

I felt his hand on my shoulder, strong. I didn't feel strong. I was filled with a well of sorrow that had no end. His silence brought my tears brimming to the surface.

"Ye were long in the cold, lad. We barely were able to bring yer body temperature back to normal. I'm sorry. It was the freezing sickness. Ye're lucky to be alive. Ye've been lost to us for many a day."

"What?" I cried, embarrassed by the wobble in my voice and the tears in my eyes.

"Yer foot, lad. It was yer foot. Ye've lost two toes on yer left."

The dark seemed to deepen, chilling my soul. The tears I'd been pressing away escaped to rush down the sides of my face. *I was my da's runner.* The thought repeated over and over in my mind, louder with every pass. "No," I said. "No, no, no. It cannot be. Why? Why to me?"

"It's not that bad, Tormod." His words were harsh. "There are many that get by with far worse. We were able to save both o' yer feet. Ye have two strong legs. Ye will adjust. It will take some time. I'll not lie to ye, it will pain ye for a good long while."

His words barely cut the fog in my mind. I had done nothing to cause this, but it didn't feel that way.

I want to go home. I want my mam. I want to be left alone. I want my foot whole. I shouted at him deep in my mind but not aloud. His hand slid from my shoulder to my arm. I pulled away and huddled in the corner of my pallet. He hesitated and then left quietly. Cassiopeia leapt back onto the bedding and curled up near my head.

DARK BEYOND THE STORM

The Templar left me alone that night with a strong tea of willow bark to dull the pain. I didn't want to see him, and yet I did. I was angry . . . at everyone and everything — at Seamus, at God. *I prayed to Ye nine times a day. How could Ye do this to me? Why?* I railed. *I saved him. I should have been rewarded. Why have Ye punished me instead?* It was bad, all of it. But what was worse was there was a small part of me screaming that the Templar knew it was going to happen. He had the vision sense. I could not help but wonder if he had seen it days ago. I was confused. I had never been able to change the future — what I *saw,* happened — but what if he could, and he didn't?

I slept to escape all that had happened. My dreams were terrible. I ran in them, not happily with the wind at my back as I once would have, but jerkily, and forever chased by something or someone pounding heavily behind me. I woke several times in the night, the last when the Templar came to check on me, but I was not yet ready to face him.

A full day and night passed before I had the strength and courage to peel back the dressing. The sight of my bloody foot made me retch into the chamber pot by my bedding.

"Go easy, leanabh." I knew that he had entered, for the draft from the open door made the light of the candle flicker. As the last of the heaves and tremors passed, I leaned spent against the pallet's edge and took the cool scrap of linen he offered to wipe my face.

"It looks bad, aye, but it will heal well. Ye've got to be vigilant about cleaning the site, though. I've seen such before. Ye need to make sure that the wasting does no' progress further."

My empty stomach heaved yet again.

"I'm sorry, lad. I forget that my words might fall harshly on yer ears."

"No. I . . . 'tis all right." Though I tried to suppress it, my voice shook. I swallowed hard, willing myself to be strong. "Who has seen to me?"

His gaze met mine. "Seamus didn't leave yer side until ye woke. And even now, he'll let no other prepare the water and herbs."

Anger tore through me at the name and the thought

of my mangled foot. "He need not bother. He had no use for me. I want no part o' his guilt."

The Templar didn't even raise an eyebrow and his voice remained calm. "I'll arrange for one o' the others," he said. "Tormod, what ye did back there was nothing short o' heroic. He would surely have died had ye not thought quickly and acted as ye did."

It would have been better for me if I had not done as I had, my mind shouted. *If I had to do it again, I would not.*

"Ye do yerself a disservice, Tormod. Ye did as was right. Ye've a good heart." He spoke again as if he could read my mind. I had not the faith in myself that he placed upon me.

I could not bear to meet his eyes, to see the disappointment that would surely be there. I just wanted to be left alone. My foot was throbbing, and my mind was a blur. He stood. "Lay yer head, lad. Get some rest. We've time to talk o' it later."

I did as he bid. I could do nothing else.

✠

Horace brought the supplies for my wound care. The big man moved surprisingly quietly for the giant he was. I watched him wordlessly.

"Master Tormod, did I wake you?"

"No, Horace. I'm sorry I was added to yer duties," I said quietly.

He laughed his great barrel laugh. "An' ye're so much worse than shifting ballast."

I wanted to laugh, but I didn't have the energy. "How do I do it? Clean the wound, I mean?" Talking seemed to push away the threat of tears that came on every time I thought of what I'd lost, or what I would have to face.

"Seawater boiled with garlic bulbs and leaves o' witch hazel. Ye clean it like this." He was gentle, another surprise. "Do this for as long as ye need, but when ye feel able, soak the whole o' it."

As he spoke, he carefully showed me how to clean the wound that someone had stitched with rough black thread. The pain was so heady that I could barely hear him. My ears hummed and black crept up behind my eyes. I had no notion that my tears were running freely until I heard my own hiccupping breath and felt the dampness on the blankets. It was embarrassing.

"It will be all right, Tormod. Cry if ye need to." Fiery jags raced through the whole of my leg. I focused on the back of his neck and saw the thin white scars I'd never seen before. It was a shock. I ran one finger over the closest and he flinched.

The lash came down with savage brutality. Pain

rippled, close and hot, not within me, but an echo of a memory that still contained it.

Focus. Ground. Shield. I was back in seconds, my body trembling. Horace thought it was from the pain. Maybe it was, but I knew this pain was nothing compared to the one he had endured.

✠

The chamber was dark and it was late, but I was restless. The air shifted, and I closed my eyes to just a slit. Someone came to change the water. His bulk was not Horace. Fury washed through me. Seamus.

Silent, he stood by me. I wanted to move, to yell, to smash his face, but I couldn't. The coverlet had fallen to the floor, and I held my breath as he lifted it and laid it back on top of me. The weight was painful, but I could not afford to wince. It seemed forever before he left.

I sat up shakily, pushed aside the bedding, and carefully began to remove the dressing. It was stiff with dried blood and the sight of it was as nauseating as the last time I'd looked, but the Templar's warning made me press on.

Wasting no time on a dry wash, I inched the whole of it slowly into the bucket. The pain was heady; my body shook with it. Several moments passed before I was able to draw a breath without feeling the need to retch.

Cassiopeia came in through the open door and

began nosing around the bucket. Absently I reached down and rubbed her neck. The light of my candle sent out flickering bits of gold that illuminated a small area of my berth. I could see into the bucket. The blood had mixed with the solution and the water had turned a dark and murky red.

I could not bear to touch it yet, so I let the water do what it would. The scarlet depths of the bucket called out to me and I slipped inside.

Old and blistered feet cried out for relief. A clumsy bag pressed into back and sides. A familiar heat wafted through the thin material. The crash of a waterfall played in my ears. A myriad of sparkling lights danced before my eyes.

Focus. Ground. Shield. As I lurched back to the present, my foot burned like the devil. I lifted it from the bucket, swaying in my seat, recovering from the vision. My breath was shallow, and the room faded in and out for many moments. Cassiopeia sat on my coverlet eyeing me as though I were an oddity.

This vision was unusual. Somehow important, I knew. I blotted the wound with the edge of my plaid, barely noting the clean pink skin and dark stitches. I had to tell the Templar what I'd seen.

Replacing the old bandage with a new one, I chanced putting weight on the foot. The pain was heady and so instead I hobbled to the wall and on one foot crossed the room. The deck was empty save for the Templar, and when he saw me, he propped the wheel and hurried to my side.

"Are ye mad? Ye'll tear the stitches and have to start the healing all over again." He helped me down onto a pile of sailcloth. The short journey had robbed me of all strength and much breath. "I've had another vision.

"It was an old man. Someone from the past." The Templar's silence urged me on. "I think he may have carried the carving. I felt the heat and saw the light. 'Twas in flashes, like always, but an echo o' his thoughts was tied to the images as well. He had a responsibility, and was determined to see it through."

"Can ye recall the setting?" the Templar asked. "What was 'round him?"

I closed my eyes. I was beyond tired, and my foot was throbbing. The lap of the sea was comforting. It came to me then. "A waterfall." Sleep was calling out to me. The Templar draped a length of canvas over me and left me to return to the wheel.

SEASICK

The days that followed passed slowly. The pain of my wound continued. At times the burning came from deep inside, like my bones were spewing flames. At other times it was like a distant ache, and it was then that I felt as if the toes were still there — like they had gone to sleep and were now waking with a rush of pinpricks.

I was on deck, sitting next to Geordie, chipping away at the board nearest. My foot began to ache and I stopped working, biting my lip. "Why does it do that?"

The Templar was at the wheel. "What?"

"Hurt like the toes are still there."

"The blood is circulating in a healthy manner, rushing to the area to provide healing. I would worry if it were not doing that."

As always, the things he knew were surprising. He was not at all old, but his experience and learning were endlessly vast.

"Ye don't have to push yerself this way, Tormod," he said.

"Aye, but I canno' sit idly by; the seasickness comes on."

My stomach rumbled but I ignored it. The prospect of food had little appeal. We had long since eaten anything fresh. All we had now was a store of dried and salted beef, with an odd turnip or old onion thrown in as a treat. And with the weather so often wet or misty, we could not even use the ceramic fire pit on deck to cook the fresh fish we caught. Some of the crew ate it raw, but the thought of it made me sick. I ate what

I could but not much more. I had no appetite for anything, really. Being with people, being alone, it was all the same.

We had been at sea for a very long while. The notches in the hold had grown and grown. The horizon line where the light of the sky met the dark of the water was the only visual break, and I spent much of my time staring in its direction.

And then there was the oddness of my nights. The dreams that I had on waking from the fever seemed to have unlocked something deep inside. Every night, from that first night on, I experienced a vision while I slept, a different place, a bit of life that was not my own. They came from all over, but they had something in common — the sparkling light and heat of the carving was there.

But now, many times, there also came an aspect I began to dread. The heat I associated with the tingling warmth became at times unbearable. It was as if my body was aflame, my skin scorched.

As I worked, chips of tar scattered before my blade. *Danger.* I sat up, confused. A thickness floated on the wind, like a sour scent. I inhaled it and cringed. The sky was no longer clear and blue, but dark and overcast. My foot ached, deep inside, as if the bones were swollen. My body was tight and my mouth was uncommonly dry.

We were nearing the harbor. Several ships were anchored there ahead of us. I leaned over the rail to see. Dread rose up inside me the closer we came.

I moved toward the Templar. "Something is wrong," I said. "I feel it."

✠

"Seamus, take us wide. Horace, drop the sail." As the Templar called directions to the men below, I walked the deck keeping the ships ahead in sight. The wind whipped past me, billowing my plaid. I watched as it crossed the water, building peaks of white. My sight lifted just as the closest vessel's pennant unfurled. The image of golden lillies floated on a field of blue.

"Tormod, get back."

I ducked and scuttled to his side.

"The markings are Philippe's. We move no closer." The Templar's voice was urgent. Beneath my feet the ship pulled as Seamus corrected course.

"Follow the coast an' put in to the cove two miles on," said the Templar.

A shiver raced through me. Perhaps they had not seen us.

"We go ashore within a candle mark," he said to me. "Be ready." As he spoke, a sharp bristle of irritation crossed Seamus's face.

"I need ye here," the Templar said. "I want a careful

135

watch on the ship. No one leaves, and none enter until we arrive back. I do not intend to be long. If anyone asks why we are here, it is to take on wine from the Santa Marissima Vineyards." He didn't take his eyes off the French ship until we rounded the coast. "Seamus," he said, approaching the wheel, "if anything goes wrong an' we don't return, get a message to the Archbishop."

"Have ye seen something?" Seamus asked.

His body grew still, his eyes fading, distant, reaching for something. "It is like water, a' times as clear as day, and a' others like a murky stream."

I knew not what he meant, but thoughts of the men hunting us were more troubling to me.

The cove was small and shallow. We anchored with no fanfare or issue. The sail was lashed and the lines coiled the moment we tied off. I scrambled to my berth and dressed my foot. Much of the trip had been spent without any covering but a bandage. To go ashore, I needed something sturdier. The thought of jamming my boot over the linen bandage made me cringe, but I got on with it nonetheless. The soft hide stretched as I forced in my foot. It was tight and uncomfortable at first, but I waited it out and the ache seemed to lessen.

Cassiopeia twined around my legs. "I canno' take ye with me, Cass. I don't know what is going to happen." Deep in my body I felt hollow. "Be good, an' I'll bring ye something from shore." The words did not ring true. I could very well never see her again. I reached down to stroke her head and saw that my hand trembled.

When I emerged, the Templar turned and dropped his eyes toward my feet. "Can ye walk in those?"

"Aye. I'll not hold ye back," I said with as much confidence as I could muster.

He smiled faintly. "Ye've said as much before, an' ye didn't. We will take it, as we must."

"Perhaps he should stay behind, Alex." Seamus was at the wheel. I knew by his voice that he was not saying it because he was angry, but still his suggestion got under my skin.

The Templar forestalled my retort. "He is needed. We will get on."

Seamus said nothing and went below. Horace stood at the rail with Geordie, watching as we maneuvered the rope ladder to the lowered coracle. It was a difficult climb for me. I could barely feel the rope beneath the padding in my boot, and I slipped and got tangled up in my rush to get down. Then as my feet touched the boat, I overcorrected my balance and the coracle tilted dangerously. The Templar merely shifted his weight and righted us before we took on any water. "Go slowly, lad. We need to make haste, but not a' the peril o' a dunking."

The trip to shore was quick and yet I seemed to have

no end of difficulty. I had not reckoned actually getting onto the shore. There were far too many rocks to take the boat in close, so we needed to get out in water that was knee-high. To keep my injured foot and boot dry the Templar insisted on carrying me ashore. I thought of Seamus, Geordie, and Horace, and my cheeks burned. Though the distance was short, I felt as if every eye on the ship was trained on me.

"That was hard for ye, lad, eh?"

I blew out a breath and shook my head. "Aye. I didn't like it a bit."

IMPULSIVE GESTURES

The air was cold and damp, swirling around me in gusts I could not avoid. I wrapped my plaid tighter, willing warmth into my body. I thought of the ship we had seen, and there seemed nothing in the world that could warm me again. The Templar took the lead, saying little as we walked. I felt unsettled in a way that I was fast becoming accustomed to.

"We make for Santiago de Compostela," said the Templar. He drew his cloak up over his head and pulled it low over his eyes. I did the same with my plaid. " 'Tis the shrine of the Holy Way. I dare not take the main road. Stay close an' keep yer wits. We may have to move quickly. 'Tis a bit of a walk. Tell me if ye have trouble with yer foot."

I nodded.

Our pace was moderate. Though the Templar's legs were longer, and I was able to keep up, my foot throbbed beneath the wrapping. It was difficult not to limp, but I forced myself to do it, to stand straight and endure. I could feel the Templar's tension and I didn't want to distract him. We walked for at least two marks of the candle, across great swaths of land filled with hills and valleys. Brush and bramble covered much of the ground, catching my legs and tripping me as we walked. Without the sun I had no way to accurately gauge time, but when my stomach set to grumbling, I judged it past our evening meal. We were deep in a strangely fragranced forest by then.

I was hard put to keep the quiet he had set. I needed the reassurance of his voice. "What is that smell? 'Tis not like any o' the forest a' home," I said. The Templar grunted, as if he had not quite heard what I asked.

"I said, the scent here. Do ye know what it is?"

I thought he was going to ignore the question. His

back was as tight as a strung bow, and his eyes peered intently ahead as he walked.

" 'Tis the leaf o' the myrtle," he said quietly. " 'Tis said to have soothing properties. The scent calms the mind an' refreshes the soul."

I went quiet again, hoping against hope that what he had said was true. If there was one thing I craved at that moment, it was peace of mind. I was sick with the thought of the men hunting us.

Traveling a rough path through the forest, we avoided the main road for a time. When there was no other choice, we chanced walking where we could be seen; but as people came within hearing, we darted to the side until they passed. Many of those on the road were in far worse shape than I with my bandaged foot. Their clothes were ragged, and their bodies were gaunt. Their smell, though, was by far the worst thing about them. It was so strong at times, even from our place of concealment, that I covered my nose and mouth with the edge of my plaid and still I felt the constant need to gag.

The Templar spoke when we were once again alone. Perhaps he noticed that I needed a distraction. I jumped at the crackle of leaves and, more than once while I was looking behind, trod on his heels.

"Santiago de Compostela is the final destination o'

a holy pilgrimage an' one o' the greatest sites o' adoration in the world."

"Aye?"

"The story goes that James, one o' Jesus's first four Apostles, was beheaded by the king Herodes, who forbade the Apostle a proper burial. The Disciples smuggled the body out o' Jerusalem, loaded it into a skin boat, an' launched it on the sea.

"Wind an' the guiding hands o' the angels, they say, carried the boat safely here to Compostela. An' the people brought the body to the local queen, Lupa, who 'tis said had a vision that instructed her to give the Apostle a proper burial. She had him laid out in a great marble sarcophagus in the crypt where we head."

I nearly trampled him when he stooped and picked up something small and white from the path. He grunted and recovered his balance quickly. "A little room, Tormod."

"I'm sorry," I mumbled, moving away.

"Scallop shells," he said, looking at the bit he had picked up, "became the symbol o' the skin boat wherein the Apostles laid the body an' now represent this Pilgrimage."

I looked around. Shells littered the path we had just come upon. "They carry them with them?"

"Aye, pinned to their hats or carried in their goods."

Up ahead, the noise of a group of people alarmed me. We had not seen any for quite some time and it was loud to my ears. "Here," he said. "Come this way."

A queue of pilgrims lined up before the doors of the kirk. The Templar led me to the side, and we followed a rough trail to the back stone wall. The land was uneven. Rocks and briars blocked our path and caught our clothes as we made our way.

"Where are we go —"

He swept his arm wide, flattening me against the wall of the kirk. My breath was halting as we listened and waited. I kept my peace but wanted to shriek. Slowly, carefully, he inched the door open and silently moved inside. I followed.

We were in a room, separate from the main kirk. The chamber was completely black and as silent as a tomb. We stood in absolute stillness as the moments ticked by, one by one, until at last I could bear it no longer. "Shall I light a taper?"

My whisper was like a shout in the darkness. His hand shot out and clamped over my mouth. A quick scratch was followed by a burst of light. I shielded my eyes.

Illuminated by the flame, not three hand spans from my face, was a sight that chilled me to the marrow. We were not alone. The Templar had known it all along.

Dark eyes met mine, and they seemed to glow with an inhuman shine.

FRIEND OR FOE

The man was a terrifying sight. He was swathed in many dark and flowing robes, from his veiled head to his sandaled feet. The skin of his face was a deep brown, as if the sun had shone on him for years and toasted him crisply. His fingers were long and thin, and flowed gracefully as he touched his forehead, then chest in greeting. "Salaam, my brother. It is good to see you yet alive."

The Templar breathed out heavily, and I felt the release of tension from his body. He took his hand from my mouth with barely leashed violence. "Tormod, there are times when ye tempt my sword an' my peace o' mind mightily."

I was shaken. I'd done it again. I'd done something stupid, something dangerous, and made him angry.

"Ahram," said the Templar, grasping forearms with the man. "Ye don't know how glad I am to find *ye* here an' no' another." His glance passed over me, and I ducked my head and moved away from them both.

"We have had a watch set for many a night in hopes of your arrival," said the other. His voice had a melodic ring.

"What news have ye?" asked the Templar.

"Mercenaries scout the bays seeking a Knight Templar traveling from the north. They are most persistent in their inquiry. You cannot linger here."

My head snapped up at his words. *Mercenaries? Hired killers?*

"Tell me all," he said quietly.

"They landed two days past, and small parties have been going out at regular intervals. They've men positioned all along the road, and one contingent has moved on inland." His hand found and rested on the haft of his sword, perhaps out of habit. I stepped back a pace in case there was another reason, but he paid me no heed. "I sent men to follow the ones who went on and have not heard back from them yet."

"What direction did they take?"

"East."

The Templar's mouth was tight and furrows stood on either side. He moved to a table near the back wall and lit several tapers. I stood beyond the edge of the light, watching the stranger and wondering at the easy relationship between the two. I had always thought that Arab and Christian hated one another. Clearly these two didn't.

The Templar drew a rolled parchment from beneath his vestments and placed it on the table.

"Tormod, come here." I crossed the space slowly, looking down on what he held. It was the map I'd drawn, but set in a much larger tract of land.

The Templar spread the parchment and bade me hold two corners. He held the others and began tracing a path with his finger. "We must travel here," he said.

The dark man moved closer into the light to look, and I sucked in a breath. A series of strange runes were inscribed in the skin of his cheek. He felt my stare and turned to me. I was startled by the near total blackness of his eyes.

A white mantle stirred. The sound of battling swords cut the air. Black eyes flashed as blood splashed dark runes.

Focus. Ground. Shield. I barely remembered the commands, so strong was the vision. As it winked out, I wavered, backing away from the man, my eyes still locked with his. He said nothing, turning to the map.

"Tormod, the map," reminded the Templar. My eyes beseeched him, but either he didn't notice or chose not to act on it. I reached out once again and held the edges, carefully avoiding contact with the Arab. I needed to tell the Templar he could not trust the man at our side, but I could say nothing.

"We have reasoned that these markings here are stars that are set in the sky as it appears over this land. They will appear clearly during the July moon. Using those calculations, I place the map's destination here — beyond the mountains, deep in the Languedoc. Have you been in this region?" he asked.

"I have not. It is not a place that would welcome our kind," said the Arab.

"Ye should be welcome in all lands," said the Templar.

The Arab dipped his head in acknowledgment. "The ports are patrolled," he said. "You will best be served moving across the land."

The Templar stared, thinking. "Aye, perhaps," he replied. "We must move quickly, an' those seeking us must be diverted. I'll send my men on ahead by sea. If chased, they should be safe enough without my presence. The enemy seeks a Knight Templar an' entourage. Seamus does not wear the white as yet. I would ask that ye take yer men to the ship an' tell Seamus the plan. We will move on as pilgrims. Keep watch for us at Ponferrada. We travel the Holy Road."

"May Allah watch over you, Alexander. You seem to have more enemies than friends these days."

"I'll be pleased to have His protection."

The Arab left, with a cursory glance that passed over me. I was glad of it. We stayed only long enough to reroll the map and douse the candles. A storm was building. The air fairly crackled with energy.

"We go on alone, Tormod. How fares yer foot?" he asked, climbing the bank of dirt behind the kirk.

It ached, but I was too caught up in my worries to dwell on it. "I'm well," I said. At the top of the slope, we quickly angled east over a meadow of tall grass. Night had fallen while we were inside. The damp from the rain seeped into my boots and in moments it was fair uncomfortable, but I said nothing.

"Ye're excessively quiet," he said after a while. "Let it go. Ye need not obsess about it every time I snap at ye, Tormod." His voice was peevish.

"No, I'm not. Speaking out when I did was a stupid thing to do, an' I will try not to do it again, but that's not it." I suddenly felt unsure about telling him what really bothered me.

"Ye had another vision, while we were inside," he guessed.

He had recognized the signs. "Aye. An' I feel that I must tell ye, though I know ye don't want me to."

He said nothing.

"Beware the man with the runes," I said. "Danger an' pain surround him."

"In this ye're mistaken. Ahram is like my brother. I would trust him with my life."

"Then ye throw yer life away!"

I cringed expecting another reprimand, but instead he said, "Good to see ye returning to yerself, Tormod. I thought ye had lost yer spark with yer toes. But that is enough."

It was said with a quiet authority. I shut my mouth then. We walked for a moment in awkward silence. I asked, as much out of curiosity as out of the need to get back on a solid keel with him, "Will they find us?"

"I'll do my best to protect ye, Tormod. I pledge that on my life."

It was not a guarantee, but I felt all the better for it.

REST AHEAD

We worked our way across the land in near silence and constant watchfulness. Keeping far from the main paths, we skirted the villages when we came on them. The Templar's pace was quick, and I struggled to stay abreast, or at the very least, right behind him. My foot burned with the unaccustomed exertion, but I didn't complain. I had no idea where we were headed, but it was clear that we needed to arrive, wherever it was, in great haste. It took all the willpower in me, but I didn't initiate conversation. He was troubled, and though I would have liked to think I could help, I knew that I could not.

It was late when he broke the silence. "The Order has safe houses scattered throughout the Continent. We will make for one I know. 'Tis just beyond a league from here. Can ye bear it? We dare not stop. They are close. The carving is glowing in the depth o' my sporran. I can feel the heat. There is danger."

I craned my neck around, sure that they must be waiting behind the next bush. The constant ache of my foot until then was not so tremendous that I could not put it out of my mind, yet the moment he mentioned it, the pain seemed to come on doubly. "I am well enough," I said, gritting my teeth as I stumbled over a snarl of roots at my feet.

He looked on my pinched face with doubt. We had been traveling through a thinly forested area. Around us now were many stripling trees. He took his sword from its hilt and hacked at one of the dry limbs. "We will clean it properly later, but for now use this to support some o' yer weight. 'Tis not much, but the best I can offer at the moment."

It was awkward and no help at first, but after a while I was better at making the stick and leg move in unison. It didn't, however, take away the pain. I felt more tired and weak as the night progressed. The moon remained behind a dark scud of cloud, and I stumbled often.

"Rest is not long away." His voice was harsh, and I felt ashamed for my weakness, as if I had failed the faith he entrusted in me.

"Ye mistake my mood. Ye're recently arisen from the sickbed and ye cannot be expected to travel this way. Yet ye must."

I wanted to keep on, to live up to his expectations, but I was having trouble keeping the ground before my eyes steady. We moved deeper into the forest. The trees grew dense, and in the darkness my eyes and legs were uncertain.

The moon slid from its place in the clouds just as we came on a croft set near the base of a steep grade. It was so like home that for a moment I slowed.

I could well imagine that off to the side in a paddock were sheep and a goat. And in the morning a rooster would strut with great purpose across the rocky lane that led to an old stone hut.

The Templar read my mood. He said nothing of it, but nodded to me.

At the crude wooden door, he knocked a strange pattern. An old woman peered out with pale and wary eyes, seeking his features within the hood.

I was surprised when he pushed back the cowl. He had been so careful during our travels. The woman started visibly and quickly sketched the sign of the cross. Then, with a rapid-fire burst of speech in a language I didn't understand, she took both his hands in hers.

"Aye, Marta. It is truly myself." He laughed; his smile was warm and wide. I found myself smiling as well.

We were quickly drawn inside and I was directed to a mat before a central fire. I stumbled to it, scarcely keeping my eyes open. The woman drew a bowl of stew from the heavy pot hanging from the ridgepole. The smell of the soup, and the scent of the wood burning beneath, again struck in me such a longing for home that my eyes teared. I ate quickly, swallowing over the lump in my throat, and finally lay down. The buzz of their conversation lulled me, and I gave in readily to sleep.

The Templar woke me before the sun began its ascent into the morning sky. "Our presence here will not go unnoticed. We dare not stay 'til nightfall." It was a small phrase, but it brought me awake, though I felt I had just gone to sleep.

"I thought it was safe. They'll look here?" I mumbled.

"Aye, but perhaps not for a while."

I rubbed my eyes, pushing aside the sleep that still tried to claim me. Sitting up slowly, I looked around, barely remembering the room.

"Here. These will give ye a start." He set a platter of lush blue-black fruit between us.

"What are they?"

"These are grapes, Tormod. Marta has a large vineyard behind the hut. She and her family harvest the fruit an' make wines an' juice from them. They supply the priories of France an' Spain."

"Would that not take more than a small single family?"

He smiled. "Aye. But Marta's family is not small. Her husband, God rest his soul, began a partnership with the Templars. Marta runs it now with the help o' her sons. Many o' our knights, sergeants, an' apprentices work for a time in the vineyard an' winery. Do ye recall the fields o' vines we have been passing through?"

I nodded.

"Did ye feel a shift in the life o' the land?"

I had noticed the change. We had moved from waving plains of wheat to lush and verdant fields of tangled vines.

"Aye. The life's beat is deeper. 'Tis like a different resonance strummed beneath my feet an' in the air."

"Aye. The land is ancient. All o' this is Marta's. There are hundreds o' acres o' vines an' a small town just beyond the hills to our west. Marta lives out here in her modest hut out o' preference, with one or two o' the men looking in on her."

"So how do ye know each other?" I asked.

"I apprenticed here for a time," he said, stretching his feet out in front of him.

It pleased me to imagine the Templar toiling among the vines, an image even more fitting than that of him in full battle regalia. The more I knew of him and of the Templars, the more conflicted my picture of them became. Nothing was as black-and-white as I had thought. I was slowly beginning to understand the Order through him, and the more I knew about them, the more I wanted to know.

"Did ye rest at all?" I asked unable to restrain the yawn that stretched my words.

"I did," he said.

I didn't truly believe him.

"Here, change into these." For the first time I noticed that he was wearing the plain brown serge robe of a peasant. He had given me one as well. "We will travel out in the open with a group returning from the pilgrimage. They are staying a' the main house by the winery an' leave shortly."

Rested by the night's respite, I shrugged into the

foreign clothes. My robe was old and a bit large, but its well-worn surface felt soft on my skin, and the drape was less heavy than my plaid. I felt silly in the old straw hat, but the Templar insisted it would be valuable both as a disguise and as a way to keep the heat off. To complete my look, he draped my neck with a beaded crucifix of wood.

"Take off yer boot an' clean the wound in the bucket outside. Then wrap this around before ye put it back on." He handed me a bundle of soft fur, the hide of a rabbit.

Outside, the morning air was chill and damp. There was a well down behind the house, from which I drew a bucket of cold water. Sitting on the ground, I set to it.

The hide of my boot had stretched with the extra padding and it slipped off easily, but the interior of the linen was dry and stuck. My stitches had not fared well. Some had torn and bled. The skin around them was red and irritated, and it burned now that the bindings were off. Quickly, before I lost my nerve, I poured water over the injury. Pain flooded my mind with waves of heat.

The Templar came out moments later. "Here, this ought to help as well." He had stripped the bark from a strong limb. A much sturdier stick, already dried, hardened, and more than likely used before, leaned against the well. I stuffed my plaid into a sack of supplies and adjusted my robes to match his, keeping my sporran beneath.

He seemed fully ready to leave. "We will travel weaponless?" I asked.

"Not entirely," he replied. "I will have knives, an' ye, yer dagger, an' o' course my sword still sits in its place." He shifted the straw hat to reveal the hilt. The rest lay hidden beneath his robe. "Still, it would no' be easy to get to this way, so . . ." He pulled his staff apart and a thin wicked blade gleamed in the half-light.

"God's breath!" I was astounded. "Where can I get one o' those?"

The Templar laughed. "There are times when ye're much older than yer years, an' others when I am reminded o' the lad from the village."

"Where did ye get that?" I asked, looking at my own staff to see if it had a hidden blade as well. *Nothing.*

"I made it long ago, when I was here, working." His eyes had a far-off look, as if he were remembering that other time.

Marta had laid aside some food to take with us on the journey and brought it out to us in a linen sack. I was beginning to feel the stirrings of excitement over our covert travel, a definite shift from my nerves of the night before.

I had finished washing, and my foot was packed in the soft fur. My boot slid back on snugly. When I looked up, I realized that the Templar's eyes had gone wide and unfocused. Almost immediately he snapped to.

"Tormod, come. We must leave. A band o' soldiers is traveling this way. They approach from the south and will be here within a candle mark. We cannot wait for the rest o' the pilgrims. The carving feels as if it will burn a hole in my sporran. We must be away, now."

The Templar spoke rapid Spanish and Marta came out of the hut, looking off down the road warily. The Templar rolled his vestments into his sack, and with a wave we were off. The ground was rough and rocky, and my foot was tired from our forced travel of the night. Still, I hurried.

As we gained the slope into the woods, a nasty chill trickled along my spine and I looked down. At the very edge of the snaking road that led to Marta's, I saw the faint outline of men approaching.

"Into the trees," the Templar said, hurrying me. "They canno' see us, but we take no chances. Do no' stop or slow to look back again."

I hurried behind him.

�֎

We traveled many leagues. Even as the sun slid from the sky once more, we continued. I was glad of the rest taken at Marta's, for even after we broke for food, we didn't make camp but continued our forced pace.

"How could they have found us so quickly?" I asked, hurrying after the Templar.

"I don't know." The answer was short and didn't brook an invitation for more. It was as if he'd sunk deep into himself, as if I was not there at all.

When at last we broke for sleep, I am fairly certain that only I laid my head. The Templar sat with his back to a sturdy rock. His broad sword lay across his knees, and though he didn't kneel or close his eyes, I heard the steady drone of his prayers.

ATTACK

A woman's cloak lay tattered on the ground. Frightened eyes plead for mercy. Cries rent my ears.

"Tormod. Wake up. It's just a dream."

I was awake, but the vision would not leave me. "Get away! Stop! She knows nothing!" I shouted.

"Focus. Ground. Shield. Push it aside. Listen." The Templar's voice was in my ears, in my mind, and yet I could do nothing to heed him.

"Leave her alone! Stop!" A blade glinted red. Her scream and mine were one.

A strange, cold thickness washed over me, enveloping my mind. I latched on to it and let it separate me from the darkness. The vision faded. But its memory lived on. Tears trickled down my cheeks.

"Shhh, leanabh. Hush ye now. Embrace the stillness. Feel the cold." I realized I was in the clearing, beneath the trees, huddled against him. My tears would not stop. Beyond my mind, I heard his instruction again. *Reach, Tormod. Distance yourself.*

I understood then and embraced the peace he was projecting. In moments I was still. My eyes dried and awkwardly I pulled away. "I'm sorry."

He left me to deal with the embarrassment of my tears, tending the fire, then bringing me a skin of water.

"Do ye want to tell me?" he finally asked quietly.

My head hurt and my heart ached. The words were slow coming, and when they came, it felt like someone else was speaking them. "Marta is dead. They killed her after we left."

His face paled and his body hunched in pain.

"I should not have gone there. I brought them down on her. She was an innocent," he said. His anguish was painful to watch.

I knew not what made me speak. I had no experience in anything of this sort, save the words my da might have uttered in the same situation to me. "Ye did what ye thought best. Ye didn't kill Marta. Those men did. It was not yer fault."

"It is," he insisted. "They will stop at nothing." All of his usual light dimmed. He looked weary and sad beyond my experience. "An' then it will end."

He moved to a nearby tree and laid his hand to the bark. "The heartbeat o' the living land will thrum no more."

His intensity was frightening.

"The communion we share with all o' the earth an' its creatures is a gift beyond measure, an' yet 'tis something foreign an' strange to those whose touch is blind. In ignorance they will destroy us. We canno' allow the nongifted to possess the carving. I have seen it."

My skin grew cold. "What do ye mean?"

"Ye have the vision o' what is to come, Tormod. I have a gift that shows me not only what is an' what will be, but also what might be. My vision is split. The Order has not seen another with a gift o' this kind."

"So 'tis as ye were telling me before. Sometimes the truth o' the future can change. Ye've seen it?"

"Aye," he replied. "One future shows the carving broken an' the land's power gone still an' silent. There are no gifted in that vision, Tormod."

It was as if I had been struck. Only recently had I learned of this Brotherhood. To know that it might be on the verge of elimination, to never again feel the life that ebbed and flowed through the land — the thought was devastating.

"What o' the other future?" I asked.

"The same world, rich in the power as never before, with a new breed o' Guardian an' a legacy that goes on. Generations will birth new generations o' gifted who will serve an' protect the life o' the land. The carving gave me both o' those visions. I believe that 'tis up to ye an' I to influence one outcome or the other. We are the pebbles — or boulders — that have been thrown into the stream."

He was exhausted, his eyes were red-rimmed and his body slumped. "Try an' get some more sleep, Tormod. We're up again with the dawn."

"I canno' sleep. Ye need it more. Let me take the watch. Ye canno' go on without rest."

I could tell he was torn, but he knew I was right in this. He sighed and took a last glance around our shelter. "Aye. Don't let me sleep more than three marks o' the candle. We must travel by night long before the sun rises."

It pleased me to know that he trusted in me enough to sleep. I took out my dagger and fisted it tightly. The vision of those men and what they had done to Marta was still strong before my mind's eye. And though I was prepared to take this watch, nothing could stop me from jumping at every sound that broke the night's stillness. They were out there looking for us.

✠

I spoke truly. There was no danger of my falling asleep on a watch with thoughts of our pursuers racing through my mind. I hadn't prayed in a long while, but needed it tonight. My prayers were not what others might think appropriate, but I didn't care. I spoke direct and made no apologies.

Lord, how could Ye let that happen to her? Why are Ye letting this happen to any o' us? I shivered with revulsion as thoughts of what happened to Marta returned. It was so brutal, the violence of it beyond imagining. She was a small old woman. *Why?*

Mine was not much of a prayer, but it was all I had. I was torn up inside — about Marta, my damaged foot, the constant need to run. The Lord had not saved any of us. Maybe there was no Lord out there at all, just the power of the land and whatever held it constant. Such a thought would have Da on me with a strap. Nonetheless, the troubling thought stayed with me all night.

I was tired when the moon began its descent. The sounds of the night — the creak of the woods and the song of the insects — were making it worse. I woke the Templar with a quiet hand. He sat up right away; he had been awake.

He knelt and began the Matins, the Morning Prayer. I yawned and dropped beside him, adding my voice to his knowing he expected it.

Shortly thereafter we set out. We ate as we walked, a handful of dried beef and cheese, washed down with water from the skin we shared.

"We will make for Pamplona," said the Templar. "Following the pilgrim route through the mountains. We must break the pattern o' what is expected. They'd not think we'd travel out in the open, an' so that is the way we will take."

My legs were tired but growing stronger each day we walked. My foot seemed to ache less, though perhaps I had just grown used to the feeling. The Templar remained quiet, deep in his own thoughts, leaving me to obsess about the men hunting us.

We traveled the land as the cold of the night hung low over the hills and valleys. And as the sun began to rise, we crested a hill that overlooked a wide dirt road.

"That is it, Tormod, the Holy Road," the Templar said.

It didn't look all that holy to me. It seemed just a road, but nonetheless I followed its snaking path with my eyes. Even as early as it was, there were travelers out and about. A thin trickle of peasants — men, women, and children alike — walked the road.

The Templar watched for movement at the road's edges and, seeing none of the hunters, deemed it time we move on down the slope. As the pilgrims grew near, we ambled from our place and trailed their group. We spoke to no one; the Templar drew his hat low and I did the same.

None of the travelers seemed to mind our joining their group. It was the way of the road. Others added to the queue as the day progressed, and eventually we were in the middle of the pack and no longer at its end.

The heat that rose with the sun was stifling, especially beneath the dark robe. Sweat dripped down my back and neck in a nasty stream. I would have given anything to throw off the peasant robe and hat and bare my skin to the air. But we could not take the chance of discovery.

There were times during the trek when the road before me wavered, but the Templar seemed to know just when to ply me with water and dried meat so that I remained upright. It was a long and difficult journey. The land was one big series of hills that dipped and climbed at steep intervals. I didn't complain, though, even when the breaks came not as often as I'd hoped.

✠

We traveled a week in their company without mishap. By then, I almost was able to forget that we were hunted. And this was nearly our undoing.

We stopped for a rest by the side of the road. I could feel the life of a small stream beyond the trees and with a skin in hand set out for it. Water trickled softly over the rocks. I bent and splashed some on my face, washing the grime of the road down my neck.

Hide. The thought echoed urgently in my mind. I spun, waiting for the attack. There was nothing, yet I crouched and made my way to the trees' edge to peer beyond.

Two men had approached, soldiers caked in the dust of the road. I searched for the Templar. He was not with the group. Reaching, I sensed him by a tree opposite the pilgrims.

An old man I had shared some of my dried beef with pointed off down the road away from the direction we had come.

The soldier leaned in threateningly. "Down the road," the words of the old man came to me as he gestured again. A burst of impatience brushed the edges of my mind. I turned toward its direction and gasped as the second soldier grabbed a child. The family had only joined us the night before. The father held the mother as she strained to go to the boy. "We know nothing!" he shouted. The soldier's blade glinted in the sun as it came to rest against the small, unprotected neck of the boy. I could hear the boy's blood pulsing in my head.

"Let him go." The Templar stepped from the safety of the trees, his hands held high in surrender. "Ye have no need o' a child. Release him, now."

A strange hum floated on the air, a high-pitched whine that hovered just at the edges of my hearing. It brushed my skin with an odd heat that made my legs weak and the inside of my head itch. The soldier holding the knife seemed unable to make a decision — until the blade against the boy's neck dropped away. *Run.* The command snapped inside my mind and that of the boy, who scrambled to the safety of his father's arms.

"*Que faites-vous?*" The first soldier shouted angrily.

"*Que?*" The second shook his head, as if he were coming out of a daze.

"*Rapidement, obtenez-le!*" cried the first. Both men charged the Templar, and I rose from my crouch ready to help. The Templar moved quickly. His upraised hands knocked away his hat, dipped over his head to the hilt of the sword, and drew in a motion that I barely marked. The first man to reach him caught the swipe of the blade deep in the crease of his neck. Blood spurted bright, and the child began to scream. The second soldier followed, drawing his sword on the run, and he and the Templar engaged. Metal on metal screeched in the still, hot air as the Templar parried and swung. The soldier's advance slowed. In moments he'd lost ground. The group of travelers scattered with cries of fear.

The soldier might have been adept in his company, but the Templar was far superior in one-on-one combat. As the man struggled, the Templar's blade descended like a strike of lightning, sliding inside his guard, sinking deep in the soldier's chest.

With a sharp cry of surprise the soldier dropped to his knees, grasping at the wound as the blood flowed from his body. Then, all at once, he fell sideways and moved no more.

The Templar approached and made the sign of the cross over both men. "Tormod," he called. "Come quickly. There will be others."

The boy's father helped us drag the heavy bodies behind some rough scrub. My legs were shaking, making it hard to move them. My robe was damp with blood. "What will we do?" I asked breathlessly.

He spoke not a word but moved quickly along the road past the pilgrims. I trailed after. None of the travelers moved to follow us, and in moments we were out of sight. When we rounded a curve, the Templar left the road. I followed. Our plans had changed.

We hiked for a long time at a quick pace. My body

was tired, but there was nothing for it but to move on. Those who sought us were close behind.

The sun slipped low in the sky, but the air remained still and stifling. I wanted to keep silent, to let him lead us and think out whatever had drawn him into himself, but there came a point when I could hold back no longer.

"How did ye do it?"

He knew what I asked. "'Tis simple, for one o' our kind," he said, raising his arms and turning his palms down as he spoke. "It only works small miracles — just a bit o' shifting o' the natural forces. 'Tis not something ye should ever rely on, but it helps in a bind." His stride remained strong, but he made room beside him on the path we'd been traveling single file. "What did ye see?" he asked, the teacher in him surfacing again.

"The first man hesitated."

"Aye. Good. Notice the small things. He was hesitant, afraid before I'd done anything."

I realized that he spoke true. The one he had approached looked leery and frightened. He was young, perhaps not long in his post.

The Templar went on. "It only worked in the moment o' surprise. It would not have done much on more than one, particularly if they were bent on coming down on us."

"But how?" I pressed.

"Hmm, how to describe it?" he mused. "Ye can sense the life o' the land, aye?"

I nodded.

"Well try an' see it in yer mind's eye. Imagine it lifting right up out o' the earth an' filling the air. Then with yer mind whisper it into the form ye need."

"What form? I don't know what ye mean."

"Well, if ye want to delay someone from acting, ye whisper a screen o' uncertainty. Ye project fear an' hesitation. It will only work if the person ye're whispering it on feels that way to start. Our gift plays on emotion — yers, an' theirs."

"And if ye just don't want them to see ye?"

"Then ye whisper a bit o' preoccupation. Ye turn their minds to something that would consume them."

"Can I do it?" I asked.

"Aye. With practice. If ever we're not on the run again, we'll work on it together."

A VISITOR

Travel for the next few days was tense but uneventful. That is if you think uneventful covers walking across leagues of land with little stop or rest, with a fear that makes you start and jump every few minutes. But, compared to what it might have been, our journey was blessedly peaceful.

And then it all shifted. On the banks of the River Sil — with the bloodred sun shimmering rays of unending heat down on us, and the water, a cool and murky brown — our quiet came to an end. I stumbled to the edge, dipping my hands and soaking my face. My body felt oddly tight, as if a string that stretched from my feet to my eyes had been wound to snapping. I shook my head to clear the haziness creeping over me.

A sea of blue-and-gold pennants snapped in the wind. Rows of silver helm gleamed.

Focus. Ground. Shield. I came to with a lurch to find the Templar stooped beside me, the carving out and awash in a gleaming light.

"Danger awaits at Ponferrada," I said.

"Ahram is seeking us," he said nearly at the same time.

"But . . ."

He said nothing, just stood and continued on through the cover of high grass that grew along the bank of the river. I followed with a lump in my throat. The carving had glowed. I saw the armies. Why would he still go there?

It was the first time I had any doubt about a decision

of the Templar. It made me feel badly, like I was breaking a trust of some kind. I kept quiet, letting him lead the way, allowing the ache of my foot to occupy the best part of my mind.

✠

We came in sight of the walls at sundown and camped in a thicket below the road. "Sleep while ye can, Tormod," he said. "I will wait for Ahram; then we'll go on to the preceptory."

Thoughts of Ahram didn't make me feel better, nor did the idea that we would go to Ponferrada when clearly we could not. I fished my plaid from the sack, needing its comfort and warmth, and by an old stump I hunkered down. I must have slept then, for I awoke to a heart beating painfully. The darkness around me was absolute. I listened for the animals native to the woods, but it was unusually quiet, not the chirp of a cicada, not the cry of an owl.

A snap of underbrush brought me to my feet, my dagger extended. I nearly embedded it in the back of the Templar before realizing he was standing in front of me with his sword held at the ready.

"Peace, Alexander." The voice was strong and I recognized it immediately.

"Ahram," the Templar said with relief, his sword dropping to his side. "What has happened?"

170

RESPITE

"Your ship has been taken. Your sergeant and a monk have been detained, but this is not the place to speak. Ponferrada is overrun with the armies of King Philippe."

The Templar seemed surprised. I was shocked by his reaction. He had held the carving. I assumed that he'd had the same vision as mine.

He scrubbed fiercely at his beard, then his scalp. "Think. Why is it that I canno' think?"

I don't know why it struck me then, but I suddenly knew without a doubt what was ailing him. The carving. When I handled it on the ship, it drew strength and energy from me. He'd carried it constantly, and I had seen his drawn look many a night as I was drowsily moving toward sleep. If I had been drained by just a few of the visions, and he was receiving them day and night, how much more affected was he? I resolved to speak of it at the first opportunity.

In the darkness I could barely see, but I keenly felt the lifeblood of men behind the Arab leader. Two, clearly guards by their solid flank of him, waited silently as he spoke. I noticed what I hadn't in our previous encounter. His English was fluent, if slightly accented.

"Come, let us be away from here."

Ahram and his men led the way. The night was black as pitch, but they moved with unerring accuracy. I was, for my part, so bone-weary that it was all I could do to put one foot ahead of the other and pray for our travel's end.

The hum of the Templar and Ahram's steady conversation played at the edge of my hearing. My foot throbbed. Rest was sparse today. I could do little more than concentrate on keeping my legs strong beneath me. And yet even that was more than I could manage.

I do not know what it was that caused me to stumble, probably nothing more than the drag of my foot, but suddenly, I was on my face in the dirt and the others had to quickly adjust their stride to keep from tromping on me. What was worse, I could not seem to rise.

The Templar was beside me at once. "Tormod, are ye all right?"

"Aye." I wanted to get up then, I truly did, but there seemed no path between my mind and my body.

"Ahram," he said. "Help me."

Between them I was somehow righted, but when I tried to shift my weight to the leg, I crumpled again.

"Why did ye not tell me it was this bad," said the Templar. I felt like a bairn being taken to task and straightened, trying to ignore the fiery jags shooting through me.

"I'm fine. I just canno' seem to get my legs to work. Give me a moment an' I'll be all right."

"No. Ye can go no farther," he said, scanning the area for danger.

"But ye canno' afford to stop," I protested. "Ye have to go on. Leave me here. I'll rest a bit an' catch up to ye."

He looked at me as if I'd grown several heads and could not tell which one was speaking. "Are ye daft? There's no way ye would ever find yer way alone."

I could not have felt worse, or at least that's what I thought at the time, but I was wrong. Staring at the face of the Templar, I realized that I was exceedingly hot. And the dark seemed to close in on me quickly. I shook my head, but it did me no good. The ground was coming up to meet me, and I could do nothing about it.

A few moments later I woke, with my body folded like a potato sack over the shoulder of one of the Arab men. My ribs felt like they'd been beaten, and my back was stretched. "Stop!" I cried. "Put me down!" My face was aflame and my nose full of the spicy smell of his body.

"We canno' do it, Tormod. We have to get ye to the next preceptory. Ye need a healer. The injury is weeping and red. If we don't care for it soon, it will not go well for ye."

"I can walk," I insisted. "'Tis true. Just let me show ye."

He moved close and said, "I'm sorry, Tormod. Ye're far from the safety o' home. I have to protect ye the best way I know."

I heard and felt his exhaustion and I held my tongue, wishing that I had never complained, never been a burden to this man already so taxed. I vowed that I would be better, do more to help, and cause him no worries.

It was hard, I tell you. Mine was not an easy transport. Even though my foot didn't hurt as much, hanging the way I was made my head feel light. I was lucky that the distance was not as much as it might have been. But better still, not long after the first man traded me to the second, I asked if I could not sit at his back with my legs and arms wrapped around.

It was strange. Though the man bore no resemblance to my da, I had a quick flash thought of doing just this, riding his back when I was a bairn. My throat quickened and my eyes filmed. As luck would have it, we came on the preceptory just when I most needed saving from my thoughts of the past.

It seemed less a preceptory than a fair-sized croft. I

slid my legs from their cramped position around the waist of the man carrying me, and the sudden drag forced him to let me down. I rued the decision straight off, as hot jabs of pain rippled through my foot. Slowly I limped to the Templar's side. He quickly put his arm around my waist to support me. "Just a bit more. I know ye can make it."

As we passed through the last of the trees, I had never felt so keenly that I'd come home. The face of the guard was not familiar, but the strong red cross on the white of his vestments brought a relief that had been long away.

We straggled up the road bedraggled and so dead on our feet that the last few steps were a pure trial. "Can ye stand?" the Templar asked of me.

"Aye," I said, and fought through the sudden wash of disorientation caused by my effort. The Templar approached the guard at the door of the manor house and spoke several words, some of which I recognized as his name.

A tall, broad-shouldered, older knight crossed the courtyard before us, eyeing our party with ill-concealed wariness. He had a strong profile and sharp gray eyes that seemed to miss nothing. Though he didn't speak, I felt power issue from him, as if he glowed with something vital, something unearthly, holy even. I could do nothing but gawk.

The Templar stepped forward. "Grand Master." His relief was obvious. "I feared never to cross yer path. There is much we must discuss." The man greeted the Templar, clasping forearms. "Well met, Alexander. I am ever your servant." His voice was like thunder before the rain. Deep, rumbling, purposeful.

There was something in their position, mayhap the posture or the light.

A rush of sound rose in my ears, the furor of a crowd bent on destruction. Against the purple of an evening sky, the billow of white robes glimmered. The red glow of a spark kindled dark wood. Smoke lifted and curled. And gray eyes flashed with anger and conviction.

I crumpled to the ground, as an all-encompassing blackness took me beyond the night, beyond the preceptory, and beyond the pain, to a peace that filled my entire being.

ABANDONED

A horrid smell filled my mouth and nose. I twisted away, trying to breathe, but it followed me wherever I moved. I shoved at it, fighting to keep from retching up whatever remained in my stomach.

"Here, here, lad. I mean ye no harm. I just need ye to wake."

I woke, but the vision that had caused me to reel hung before my mind's eye. "The Templar, Alexander, where is he? I need to see him straightaway!"

"A fellow Scot, are ye?" the healer crouched before me exclaimed. "Well, whatever ye need to speak o' will have to bide, lad. He's closed up with the Grand Master. I don't expect ye'll hear from him again tonight. And still, there is this wound we must be tending."

My insides felt a jumble. I had fainted, and the Templar had left me. Just gone off about his business as if I didn't count, or he didn't care. I had a lump the size of a stone in my throat.

"Be ye all right, lad?" The voice of the man was not familiar, but his brogue was. And this settled me a bit. I looked around for the first time. I lay on a pallet of thick straw in a room that smelled strongly of herbs. It was dim, lit only by a small oil lamp set far from me. A small man dressed in the brown linen of a monk had his back to me, and before I could reckon what he was about, he peeled the boot, and rabbit skin I had cushioned it with, clear off my foot.

"Yow, that hurts like the devil! What are ye about, man?" I tried to jerk my foot away from him.

"I know it hurts, lad. I'll be gentle with ye in just a moment, but it has to come off. Ye need tending. 'Tis raw an' swollen from yer travel." His voice had a rough lilt to it, and I responded to his authority. It was clear he was a healer, if not from his manner, then from his place of trade. I was in a stillroom. I'd seen one before in our village. All about me hung herbs and plants drying in the warmth of the room. Lined up tidily on a large, plain table were jars of various sizes, sifting screens, a mortar and pestle, and a variety of clear vials with odd-colored liquids in them.

"Bless the good Lord's bones!" he exclaimed. "Ye've sorely tended this bit. There's a story here, to be sure. An' ye but a lad, traveling far afield on foot." He spoke quickly and so much so that I would have been hard-pressed to get a word in edgewise, but I was not of a mind to speak of my journey.

"There now," he said. "That's the last o' it. Let's take a look at that foot, then." He moved to the other side of me, and I saw his face for the first time. It was a good face, strong and caring. Carefully he prodded and turned me, so as best to see by the light in the room. It took much not to flinch, but oddly enough no pain did I feel with his efforts. Instead I felt a very strange tingling from my ankle, down my foot, and into the area that was most damaged.

I looked up into his face then and gasped. His eyes were not focused. They were in the vague far-off place I knew when I was in the visions. Without knowing how or why, I let myself drift in the same manner, not looking at the man, but seeing what it was he saw. I was shocked by it.

Just as I recognized the flow of sap in a tree, I saw in my mind's eye the inner workings of my body. I saw and felt the rush of the energy he directed deep into the wound. I was astounded. Though I could not credit the fact, it was plain that he was healing the bit where my toes used to be.

His work took no more than a few moments, and I felt myself shift back into my own world as my other sense drifted away. He cleaned the area with some soap that smelled much like the plants that surrounded us. "'Tis a miracle," I whispered reverently.

"Aye," he said, not bothering to deny what he had been doing. "A gift given by God, not o' myself, ye know. I *see* that ye have the abilities."

"I have the vision," I said. Save the Templar, it was the first time I'd spoken to any about it.

"Aye. Ye have that, too. But ye also have the healing. 'Tis just beneath the surface, waiting for ye to learn how to use it." He cleaned away the bandages and the matted rabbit fur and straightened up his work area.

"I felt ye watching with yer other senses. Ye need only to be trained or to experiment. In time yer healing powers will be as strong as mine."

I didn't know what to say. *A healing gift? Mine?*

"I know from yer words that ye come o' Scotia, but I cannot place the accent. I am from Arbroath, myself."

I was reminded that I must watch my words. Still, he was obviously one of us. "I am from the fishing village o' Leith. Tormod MacLeod is my name. My mam is o' the Highlands and my da o' the Lowlands. 'Tis why I speak oddly."

"There's no oddly about it," he said. " 'Tis a Scot ye are, and pleased I am to hear again the lilt o' my home. I am Bertrand Beaton. Tell me, lad, what brings ye so far from home in such a state?"

"I am to be an apprentice. I travel now with a knight o' the Order toward the land o' the most holy." Not the truth, but I couldn't readily tell him more. He patted my knee. " 'Tis fine, lad. 'Tis none o' my affair. Just curiosity."

I let out a breath of relief and changed the subject. "How do ye know how to heal that way?"

He moved to the table to finish grinding herbs he had obviously been working at before I arrived. "Much o' it just came to me as a child. I was forever out on the shores, mending the sea creatures that washed up with an injury. We lived a ways from the rest of the world, ye know. My da was a fisher and so was I. The village was a good day's travel away." He dusted off the pestle, poured the ground leaves into a vial, and corked it.

"Then, one day, a Knight Templar appeared at our croft. He spoke to my da about me joining the Order. I didn't know then that there were others with the ability I had. Many I met later, through my training." He cleaned the work bowl and stowed it away beneath the table, then brushed his hands together and looked around his workroom. "The rest is history. I was brought to Balantrodoch and my training began. I have been all over the world and healed many o' our brethren since then. I am here now. Who knows where tomorrow, but 'tis a good life. To know that I'm doing what I love an' making whatever contribution I might is gratifying."

I wriggled my remaining toes and tested my weight on the foot. It felt so good in comparison that I did a bit of a reel. He watched with a smile.

"I do miss the shores o' home, though. I miss my ocean, my family. I hope to return someday." It was a melancholy thought, and I could relate to it well.

"I miss home as well," I said quietly. My eyes met his, and again I was surprised to see that his gaze had drifted wide. "Ye have much ahead o' ye, Tormod

MacLeod. If ye should find yourself in need, come to me, laddie. I will help in any way I can."

I didn't know what to say. It didn't matter, for just then a runner from the Grand Master arrived. "You're to come with me," said the boy. He wore the black tunic of a trainee.

A VISION WRITTEN

The room I was shown to was simple. It held but two beds, a stool, and a small writing table. Quills, parchment, and an ink bottle lay on the table, and a thick candle sputtered, giving light to the room. I was beyond tired, but when I finally lay down, I could not sleep. I had much to think on.

I knew that the writing supplies had not been laid out for me, but I moved toward them nonetheless, as if drawn. In truth I missed my shipboard studies. I dropped onto the stool and carefully began to form my letters. At first they were random, a set of practice exercises, but then, as I warmed to it, my thoughts began to slowly appear on the page. If I could not speak it aloud to any, I could at least put down on the parchment what I had seen in the vision. It was all very rough. I'd never attempted something like this.

The candle had burned down a long way when the Templar at last arrived. He moved to my side and looked over my shoulder to see what I was about. "Once stirred, the need to express yerself is a difficult thing to deny, eh?" His voice trailed off as he realized what I'd written.

"This is a part of the vision ye have already seen?" he asked.

"Aye. It begins the same, but things add to it and it becomes stronger the more I have it."

"Ye're sure it was the Grand Master?" His eyes were dark with worry.

I nodded, going back over my words, in my mind and with my eyes. I could read and write. It was such an oddity, but more it was a way to make it all real, to give credence to what was happening, and to what I'd seen.

He took the parchment and read it once more, then held it up to the flame of the candle. I watched in fascination as the flame caught and curled a bright orange. "Have a care about what ye write, Tormod, at least until this is over. I'll have to speak to him at once, but how do ye tell a man there is a possibility that he will burn alive?" He shivered.

He made to leave but I stopped him. "Ye said it could be changed," I said.

"Let us hope so, Tormod."

"Templar Alexander, carrying the carving is taking a toll on ye, is it not?"

He stood by the door, his body hunched with the knowledge of what he had to tell the Grand Master. "Aye, ye know it rightly. 'Twas not so in the beginning, but as the visions continued, and we moved across the land, 'twas as if 'tis a full-time trial."

"I felt that way on the ship when I used it to *see*. But, as I've not held it directly for a bit, I'm stronger. How would ye feel were I to carry it a bit o' the way for ye?" I didn't want to seem impertinent. It was truly a powerful talisman, and it was his to carry, and yet he was so very tired.

He ran his hand over his face and stretched. At my words he looked over at me, considering. "Aye. I think that I'll take ye up on the offer. The carving is not something that would ever harm us. I feel that strongly. But sometimes the visions it shows, and the strength it takes to see them, are a bit overwhelming. We'll leave it be for tonight, for here. With what I've just heard from the Grand Master, I'd like to see if aught comes o' my dreams. More is happening than we knew."

His words didn't bode well for us. "What?"

"Pope Clement has of late been in conference with King Philippe. They were friends as boys. There are rumors that the Papacy is moving from Rome to France."

"What?" I exclaimed. "That is just . . ."

His gaze was far away. "Disturbing."

"What do we now?"

"We follow the map and find out what lies a' its end." He stretched and yawned. "How is the wound?" he asked. "Are ye fit to travel?"

It hit me then, that I had not told my other news. "I am healed," I said proudly, and with an awe that had not diminished. "Did ye know that some o' the gifted have the talent and are able to do that?"

I took off my boot and he came over to examine my foot. The toes were still missing, but the site of the incision was completely healed, as if years had passed, not weeks.

"I had heard tales but never witnessed it firsthand. That is truly wondrous. Ye're blessed, Tormod, to have been touched by the miracle."

"Aye. And what's stranger still is that I have the possibility to heal within." I said this last, expecting disbelief. After all, I really didn't credit it myself.

He raised his eyebrows in surprise. "Aye? What a boon that would be. We cannot stay and look into yer training, but when we return, we shall see to it."

A cold shadow drifted across my mind. A strange part of me felt that he should have said *if* we return, but I left that unsaid.

We knelt for the Compline, and though I was still very angry with the Lord, I took comfort in it. Way in the back of my mind I asked Him to make it so, to let us return, together to live out this tale. I wasn't sure I believed that He was listening, but it was important to ask.

I didn't see the Templar for the remainder of the night. He left for another audience with the Grand Master, and I took to my pallet and didn't stir until morning.

✠

Ahram and his men met us in the courtyard of the manor house. The Grand Master had arranged that we would have horses. I was glad of the fact that we would no longer be walking, but nervous, too, as I'd barely sat a horse a dozen or so times in my life. Still, I was given a good, sweet-natured mount, and we seemed to have an instant accord. I promised her quietly that if she would be good to me, I would surely be good to her.

The Grand Master met us in the courtyard before we took our leave of the preceptory. I was surprised when he came and stood directly before me. "We all must bear a cross, son. Let not what you have seen be yours. I have been warned. It is all that you can do. I go willingly to do the duty of Our Lord. There is a great duty that is yours, a destiny to fulfill. God grant you success, Tormod MacLeod." I trembled as he made the cross on my forehead, afraid to speak and yet . . . "It can be changed, My Lord. If only the right pebble is tossed into the stream."

He smiled. "Then Godspeed your voyage, Tormod. I pray you make a splash like none has ever seen."

✠

We set out in better shape and spirit than in a long while. The Grand Master was aware of our goals and was sending an armed contingent of knights to parlay for Seamus's and Andrus's release.

I had taken the carving from the Templar with all due reverence, and it now sat hidden in the sporran at my waist. The sun was high and hot by the barest hours of morning, so we broke for a time beneath the trees and rested.

It was scorching, even in the shade, and so with little to do I roamed, looking for signs of life at the base of the trees and in the clumps of weeds in the roots.

"Hah, I've got ye," I said, closing my hand around a brown and black gecko. He skittered and turned in my palm, looking for a way out. With none to be found, he settled into my hand. I sat beneath a tree watching his stillness. He was like stone in the way that he didn't move for long stints of time. Even when I nudged him, he refused to play my game. His eyes were a deep, dark brown. I stared at them as I ran my fingers down his soft back, mesmerized as the hilt of an old knife appeared in my mind's eye, fingers curved tight, curls of wood drifting to the ground. The drape of a robe emerges from the pale block. A strong swirl of power surrounds the carver.

Heat at my middle drew me from the vision. My hands rested on the precious bulk of the carving. I returned the gecko to his freedom and rose to find the Templar.

He was sparring with Ahram, though it was hot as Hades. Sweat beaded on my neck and trickled down my back. I could scarcely credit that they had the stamina to take it on, but such was the regimen of the knights. The Templar would no more miss his practice than he would skip the prayers that he did so many times a day.

Ahram was stripped to the waist. His dark skin stretched tight over well-defined muscles. The Templar fought in breeks and tunic. I had forgotten the odd injunction that he was not allowed to bare his skin before others. Such an odd rule.

The Arab's ability impressed me. He fought with a long, thin, curved sword called a scimitar, and he was, I was surprised to see, a true match for the Templar. I held my breath the whole time they sparred. The vision of the Templar being wounded was close and uncomfortable. Luckily nothing came to pass.

When they finally broke, I approached. "Templar Alexander, could I speak with ye for a moment?" I had grown a little more comfortable with Ahram as the morning and our travel progressed, but still was not sure how much I could safely share in his presence.

Ahram inclined his head, touched his forehead, then chest, as a salute, and went off in search of the stream.

I led the Templar away, off into the trees to tell of what had transpired.

"Truly interesting," said the Templar. "Ye don't know who it was? Were there any other clues ye might find if ye think on it?"

"Not that I can recall," I said. "But I will tell ye if I remember aught else. I have the image o' it, here," I gestured to my head. He nodded, and we went back to eat with the others.

I stooped beside a pile of kindling the Arabs had gathered. The men who traveled with Ahram had names that were new to my tongue. Bakir was a tall, very dark-skinned Basque who said little. The other man, Fakih, was shorter, but wide and strongly built.

Bakir had just returned with a brace of hare he laid on a bed of leaves. He'd skinned them before returning to camp and was cleaning sticks to use as skewers.

"Can I help?" I asked using hand gestures as well as words. We spoke different languages, but we'd begun to improvise.

Bakir motioned to the stream at our back. Fakih watched me with intelligent eyes. I'd seen all three Arab men washing by the river's edge before eating a short time past. I plunged my hands into the water, deep into the sand of the riverbank. The fine grit swished beneath my fingers, and I washed as I'd seen them do.

The Arabs were fastidious people. They'd washed more today than I had in a month. They even went so far as cleaning their fingers before they ate. It made me think on my own appearance and scent.

✠

Late in the afternoon we began again and, save a quick break for each of us to relieve ourselves, we rode straight through the evening. It became the norm after that first day. Though my legs and tailbone were sore from the exertion and I nearly slept astride, I became accustomed to the pace. We were crossing the countryside at a rate that could never be matched on foot. And I was getting fairly good at convincing my mount to listen.

The Templar resumed putting forth questions about the patterns in the sky. Ahram, I noticed, paid close attention to our conversations, asked his own questions, and provided some of the answers I could not. I found, during these travels, that it was becoming increasingly difficult to reckon the man, who the Templar had obvious fondness for, with the killer I had seen in my vision. He seemed to accept me readily enough, though his quiet intensity unnerved me. Of the men tracking us, we had no indication, until we entered a village on the outskirts of Bembibre.

It was the smell that warned us.

THE MESSAGE

The waft of charred thatch and the strange smell of something roasting met us halfway up the lane. We saw the farmhouse, or what was left of it.

Partial walls of stone were all that remained standing, and a small blackened tuft of thatch hung at a sharp angle near the hut's entrance. I felt the old man's grief pulse in the wind before the others noticed. He stood so still and silent that he was hard to make out in the growing dark of evening. The Templar noticed my look and turned. The closer we came, the more I could see. Before him lay a freshly mounded grave. An old sword had been thrust in the ground beside.

I slid from my horse, grasping the reins as my legs nearly buckled. The Templar had no such problem and approached ahead of the rest.

"Go away," the man murmured as we came closer. "Leave a man to his grief."

"We have no argument with ye, sir, nor wish to disturb yer mourning," said the Templar. He approached with his hands wide, showing no weapon or threat.

"Like the others," he said. "I thank you, no."

"What others?" asked the Templar. "Truly, we mean ye no harm."

The man looked at us with lost, frightened, but very angry eyes. "My son is gone. Gone! Do you hear me! My home is in ashes. There is nothing here for you." He rose and drew the sword from the ground beside him. I took a step back, out of the way, and my head began to buzz.

Large blue eyes stared with fright. The tines of a pitchfork gleamed in the blaze of a torch. The crackle of fire played in my ears. Smoke filled my nose.

Focus. Ground. Shield. I blinked, trembling.

"Be at peace, old man," said the Templar. "I can see yer pain. I know yer loss. We will trouble ye no further."

I could feel a strange ripple in the air as he spoke, as if the life beat of the land had become the gentle lap of the sea. The man's eyes seemed to dim and lose the fire of his anger. The sword dipped toward the ground.

I felt the Templar's power, and I reached as he had described to me. I added to his sway, keeping the man quiet and docile.

"How many, and how long ago?" the Templar asked. I watched and listened to the way he used the power. The old man's eyes filled with tears and he sat heavily back down. "Fifteen or more soldiers rode in two days past. They wore the colors of France."

"What business does the French king have on Spanish soil?" asked the Templar, though we knew well already.

"They seek travelers." His red-rimmed eyes narrowed and turned my way. "A Knight Templar and a young boy."

I sucked in my breath, helpless to the quiver that gripped my spine. They knew of me.

"What happened?" The Templar approached the man and knelt at the end of the grave.

"He was my son," the man said quietly. "No man should bury his son." His grief was overwhelming. It made me want to drop down beside him and beg his forgiveness. I was stunned suddenly by a thought that robbed my chest of breath. *How would my da feel if this adventure should turn out in like? It was a mistake,* I thought, *to come here — a horrible, terrible mistake.* I must have made a noise or my face gave me away for the Templar looked up. There was sadness in his eyes as he turned away and began to pray. I knew what to do without even thinking on it, and I embraced it as I hadn't before. The ground was hard beneath my knees as I dropped beside the two men and joined the prayers for the soul of the boy who had died in my stead.

Finally, it was done. We stood, lost in the quiet of the moment as crickets and cicadas filled the night air with their song.

"Come away with us," the Templar said quietly. "There is nothing for ye here."

"My home is here," the man replied. And nothing we could say would sway him from his course.

In the end we moved on, but it was with the promise that we would send men to help him rebuild when we reached the next contact house along the way. I looked back over my shoulder twice as we left. The old man stood where we had left him, with a trail of tears flowing down his weathered cheeks.

✠

We ate beneath the stars that night. The men seemed much as they had been of late. Perhaps they were used to seeing people burned out and mourning, but I was not. When I took my rest, safely beside the Templar, I could not stem the series of images that played again and again in my mind. It was worse when finally I closed my eyes. The images were freed to grow, and fear surrounded me.

I saw them in order, as if they were slowed. First, Douglas, as the arrow pierced his throat, falling forever beyond my reach; then Marta, in terror, being flung from one soldier to another, her dress in tatters, her body cut and bleeding. I saw the old man then, and then the son we had been too late to help. I saw the fear in the son's eyes.

And then came the worst. Flames surrounded the wood, licking the pitch. Smoke spiraled up past a white robe, singeing the red of the cross. I saw the face of the Grand Master, white and filmed with a layer of sweat and dust. I saw the movement of his lips. I felt the cadence of his prayer.

The image of the carving came to me in a bright white light. A woman smiled. Her eyes of deep amber held mine. The vision faded before I even had time to focus, ground, and shield. I woke with the woman fresh in my mind — her image, not as a carving, but as flesh and bone.

✠

I must have stirred or made some sound to alert him, for his eyes were on mine a short distance away in the dark. "What did ye see?" The Templar's voice was a quiet question that didn't travel beyond my hearing.

"I saw a woman, the model for the carving."

He said no more and just closed his eyes. I rolled to my back and stayed awake for a long while, staring at the stars.

THE PATH TAKEN

We rose early and wasted no time in clearing the camp of signs that we had been there. A renewed vigilance had once more taken hold. The soldiers were two days from us. It was vital that we move on and do it quickly. Our best hope lay in the belief that they were ahead of us, not behind.

The Templar was quiet, more watchful and rested than I had seen him in many days. As we made our way across the gradually changing landscape and up into the mountains, all of the men were in a state of alertness. Swords were palmed at the slightest sound, and no one initiated conversation beyond what was necessary.

The hills were rocky and travel difficult. What began as a gentle climb, a slope that crept forever upward toward the clouds, eventually became a steep grade. We led the horses and walked, sometimes singly, sometimes abreast. Footing was precarious.

The higher we climbed, the more excited by the view

I became. As we crested the rise, I sucked in a deep breath. Down below, a deep green valley lay on either side of the path. Up ahead, a thin track skirted the mountaintop.

"If we take the safer path down below, we are sure to run into the soldiers," the Templar said. "Ahram, ye've come this way before, how dangerous is it?"

"The winds are high at this time of the year. If there were another way, I'd not risk it," he said.

But we all knew we would risk it, for just this morning we had come across the evidence of a fire pit still warm from the night before. It could have been any traveler, but it had the feel of those hunting us.

"With care, and Allah on our side, we can only hope," said Ahram.

God, Allah, Jesus, or whatever Yer faithful name Ye, I thought, *if Ye would, please help us.* It was strange, but I didn't feel it was blasphemy to speak to the Lord in that manner. I knew now that there were many ways to worship the one God, and that there were many people doing it happily in all those ways.

We took nearly the whole of the night to make our way up the first steep grade, then down across the floor of the valley, and back again up the next monumental hill. And as if Mother Nature had planned it for me alone, we reached the pinnacle as the sun rose with coral fingers of light that banished the dark of an evening sky.

One by one we stepped out onto a path no wider than two men stretched lengthwise. The drop on either side seemed to careen down hundreds of rock-strewn ledges. The view was amazing. I felt as if I were on top of the world, looking down. Below me the land once again resembled the map I had seen.

"Have a care, Tormod. I dare not walk beside ye. Hold the reins tightly, and keep her head down."

We had tied a strip of linen across the eyes of our mounts, so that they would not spook and bolt. Even still, the horses twitched nervously, sensing the danger of the road before them. Ahram went first, tethered and followed closely by Fakih. I stepped out next with the Templar behind me. Bakir trailed.

Slowly we walked, leading the horses one behind the next as if it were any other narrow road at any other time. But as we neared the center, something suddenly began to change. The wind that had barely stirred the dust of the path rose in intensity. At first it was welcome for we were hot and sweat-filmed from our ascent; but when it began to blow in earnest, it stirred the birds that were below us.

I know now that I should have been holding the reins tightly, but a movement down below caught my attention and my mind wandered in its direction. It was a hawk winging slowly upward. As I watched, it caught the breeze and shot up, sweeping low over my head. I heard the flap of its wings and the scree of its cry and flinched.

My horse, already nervy, bumped against me and knocked her blind askew. I tightened my grip on the reins as the terrified creature began to back away from the edge it could see, crowding me toward the ledge it could not see. I tried to turn her, but the horse was too frightened and was heaving and shying.

"Tormod!" It happened so fast that I could not even formulate a plan. I heard the Templar's cry but could not make my mind grasp his meaning. He could not possibly want me to let go. I held the reins as the horse began to rear up and shifted my body to her side. The wind tore across the ridge. I felt the press of it against my body, pushing me. My balance was not what it should have been, and when the back legs of my mount slid off the road, the only thing I thought about was saving her, and so it was a complete shock when we both went over the side.

HELP FROM BEYOND

The bite of the rope seared like a brand, and in shock I let go of the reins. I hit the side of the cliff with such force that the breath was knocked out of me. Horror filled my mind as I watched a slide of rock follow the screaming animal down the side of the mountain. Huddled against the cliff, I tried to push it out of my mind.

I heard the men above shouting and trying to calm the rest of the horses. My rope jerked, and I dropped a bit lower. "Brace yer feet, Tormod," the Templar cried.

But I could only stare at the rock face, holding the rope that was tightening more and more while I hung. All around the life beat of the land and air swirled furiously in my mind.

"Tormod, ye need to help us!" The fear in his voice cut through, jerking me from my own terror. I would not cause him more grief. I could not. I brought my legs up and scrabbled for a foothold, using my hands to ease the slack on the ever-tightening rope. Slowly as they pulled, I clawed my way upward. But my thoughts kept drifting far below with the animal that had been entrusted me.

Tormod, feel the rock. He spoke directly into my mind, distancing me from my sorrow and pain. I focused on the shape beneath my boots, reaching with my mind to find the niches my feet could not. But rock was different. Its life beat was slower, more difficult to decipher. The carving in my sporran burned at my middle as tears dropped from my cheeks and chin, falling to the earth far below. The task seemed impossible, but suddenly I felt the beat and I understood the shape and feel of the ledge. My feet found purchase that I could almost swear was not there before. Slowly I began to climb. It seemed like forever that I made my way upward, and even longer before I was hauled back onto the cliff. The Templar was the first to draw me to my feet. I felt him shaking as we grasped arms. "I thought we'd lost ye, Tormod." His eyes were dark and worried. "I've got things to do, an' I don't intend to do them without ye!"

For the remainder of the descent out of the mountains and into France, I didn't speak. I mourned the loss of my mount, a good, spirited horse whose only mistake was to be assigned to me.

THE CHANGE

"Ye've been quiet o' late, Tormod. I would share yer thoughts, if ye'd have it." I had moved away from the group after our midday repast. I sat on a deep rock sharpening the blade he had given me. No others were within hearing. He had made sure.

"I can feel the change," I said. "Something is building. There is tightness within me. My stomach, my bones. I know not what this feeling means. Best I can describe it is when Torquil an' I are readying for a brawl. There are no solid reasons, but I know that something will spark the flame an' by the day's end I will be on my back with his fists planted in my stomach."

He nodded, a slight smile lifting the corners of his mouth at my comparison. "I feel it as well. A discord is vibrating along the channels o' our power."

"The visions are coming more often," I said. "The carving is glowing dimly. 'Tis been this way since we came over the mountain. This land is dangerous. I feel the warning."

"We must travel day an' night for a while. Just to put some distance between them an' us. I feel the presence o' our seekers more clearly than before."

✠

We didn't delay getting back on the road. The fire was stamped out and the ashes distributed so that none would see we had been in this place. The enemy was close.

How close we didn't realize until almost too late.

The sun had not yet risen. We had been traveling for much of the night and had crossed into France many marks of the candle before. Our destination was a deserted wayfarer's hut deep in the hills beyond Tarbes. We pushed our mounts and ourselves to make it, and I was very nearly asleep in the saddle. Fakih and Bakir were sharing a mount today. I had Fakih's mount and rode behind Ahram when suddenly a strange ripple of awareness shot along my spine.

Before I could alert anyone, the Templar's warning broke the stillness of the night. "Arm yerselves and make for the trees. Protect the lad a' all cost."

"Look to yerselves," I cried, drawing my dagger and kneeing my mount with fervor. I was no hero, but I refused to add yet another life in trade for my own. I raced for the darkness of the trees ahead.

I heard the clash of steel behind me. Close by my side I felt and heard the thunder of horses. A scream of pain split the air, and I wheeled the horse, terrified. The earth seemed to rumble beneath me as the overburdened mount of Fakih and Bakir went to ground. I pulled hard and circled wide, determined to help the men who were now on foot in combat.

"Ride for the trees, Tormod," the Templar commanded. "Now!"

He had never used that tone with me before, and every instinct in me wanted to obey. I started forward.

Ahead, I saw the darkness of the trees, their trunks spaced far enough apart that I would be able to enter at my rapid pace, but beyond its edges lay an eerie dark. I slowed the horse, chancing a glance behind. There were none following. I pulled up on the reins and wheeled my mount in a close circle. Ahram and his men were heavily engaged with a group of fighters. None wore French colors, and yet these men *felt* familiar. These were the same men who had been at Marta's.

An unholy anger came over me then, as I saw in my mind's eye what they had done to her. I kneed my mount back the way I'd come with only my dagger as a weapon. The Templar was before me, fighting his way toward Fakih and Bakir who fought valiantly on the ground. His broadsword cleft the air — the ring of its metal just one clang in the din of the skirmish going on all around. Ahram was engaged with two others.

The men on foot were helpless against mounted soldiers. They would be run down. As I watched, a man came at Bakir from behind. I threw my dagger, just as the Templar had taught me.

LIFE AND DEATH

With absolute accuracy my dagger caught the soldier moments before his swing came down on the unprotected back of Bakir. My blade landed square in the attacker's chest. I was shocked at the blood that spurted and could not force myself to retrieve my weapon. As the man reeled in the saddle, the Templar drove his horse at him and plucked my dagger free.

Wheeling in my direction, shouting with a fury that I could not ignore, he commanded, "Ride!"

I circled my mount once again and sprang for the trees, but not before I saw that Ahram had gotten himself between the soldiers and his men.

I entered at full speed. *Feel the trees,* the Templar commanded. His voice nearly shouted impressions inside me. In my mind I saw the aura of the trees.

I understood. Reaching, I felt for the lifeblood of the trees and fed the information directly into the legs of my mount. We flew then, unencumbered by lack of sight, with no one following our charge.

But no one could keep up the pace my mount had set. I rode for a good mark of the candle before I began to slow. The horse was frothing and my heart was beating furiously. The only sound in the forest was the birds, chirping as if nothing in the world could disturb their happiness.

I had left all of the men behind — the Templar, Ahram, Fakih, Bakir. I wanted to turn back, to help, to find out what had happened, but I knew that I needed to obey him, especially this once. I had the carving. If no one else survived, I must find a way to follow the map to discover what lay at its end.

As the sun began its quiet ascent and the darkness of the wood lifted, I found that I didn't have to focus my attention on directing the horse through the trees. I could see, as could my mount. It was then, when my attention was free, that the reality of what I had done crashed down on me.

I had killed a man. A stranger. I took a life.

I stopped the horse and stumbled toward a tree and was sick at its roots. I saw again the dagger as it flew from my hand. I saw the blood spurt and heard the man's scream. My breath rasped and I felt faint.

The Templar's horse pounded through the trees with dead accuracy. When he neared me, he vaulted from the mount, apparently not caring that the horse might run. He was in a rare fury. I found myself backing up against the tree.

"Tormod MacLeod, what in the seven hells did ye think ye were doing back there!"

I flinched from his roar. "I didn't mean —"

"O' course ye didn't mean! Ye never mean!" He was pacing and shouting. "I told ye to ride! Ride, an' no' turn an' throw the only weapon ye had on yer body. Now, I know well why yer da beat ye! Ye drove him to it!"

I could not take one moment more. "I did my best! I could no' leave a friend behind, just to save my own skin. I'm sorry, ye asked too much o' me!"

I could not believe what I had just done. Shocked by my own action, and afraid that he might tan the skin right off of me, I turned and ran like the devil himself was on my tail.

He took off right after. I should have been able to outrun him, but I had just vomited and he had anger on his side. He caught the back of my robe and yanked, and I flew off my feet. His impetus took us both to the ground where we lay heaving and crumpled.

"Tormod."

I tried to squirm to get away.

"Hold," he commanded. I shook, sure now that he would beat me. "I'm sorry."

I could not believe my ears. "What?" I gasped.

"I'm sorry ye had to go through that. 'Tis more than ye should bear."

I was horrified that he thought he needed to apologize to me. "No, I'm sorry. I knew that I had the carving. The most important thing was that I take it far from the conflict. It just happened so fast, an' I saw that man going for Bakir. An' I just could no' ride away." I buried my head beneath my arms, ashamed as tears filmed my eyes. "I killed a man. I can scarce believe it."

He rolled to his back in the brush. "To kill is never an easy task," he said. "Ye saved his life. Ye did what was right for a friend, and what's more, ye did what was right for a Templar. A Templar never runs from a confrontation, and he never leaves a man behind."

I should have felt pride in his words, but instead I felt hollow.

"Is it always this hard to bear?" I asked, tears choking my throat.

He nodded. "Each life taken is a toll on our own. I wish that I could tell ye otherwise or give ye a way to somehow make it acceptable. But that is something that must come from within. Ask for His forgiveness, for all life has come from the Maker."

I was silent a moment as we got to our feet and made our way back to the horses. They were peacefully grazing as if nothing had happened. "How are the others?" I asked. "Why are they not with ye?"

"They fare well, considering how many we took on. Fakih was cut. They are taking him to the closest village for tending. Ahram knows our path. If he can come, he will." We remounted and once again we were off on our own.

⚜

Near the height of midday we came across an abandoned wayfarer's hut tucked away in the midst of a deep wood. I was nearly overcome with heat and swaying in the saddle. My robe was stuck to me and my back was burning from the sun. We hobbled the horses in the shade by the hut and entered.

It was a small place, no more than a box of stone, with a mound of old straw, the remnants of a crude shelf that was used as a table, and several low benches. Inside was dim, and only slightly less hot.

" 'Tis too hot to hunt and there's no stream about, so let's just rest. Chew some o' these." He offered a small pouch filled with oats and a skin of water. It tasted terrible, but filled the hole in my stomach.

"Where next?" I asked, working to mush the oats with a sip of the brackish water.

"We make for Montségur. 'Tis a castle preceptory o' the Knights Hospitaller," he said.

"I've heard the name Hospitaller, but I don't know much about them. Why do we go there?" I asked, tossing off the hat and robe, fishing out my plaid, and dropping down on it.

"They are a sect like ours," he said over a mouthful of oats. "But where our knights are pledged to fight for the pilgrim's safety in the Holy Land, these are pledged to help find cures for the ill, an' provide refuge an' shelter for the sick an' injured. They're no' much in the way o' fighters, though they've been named as such. We go there for time — to rest an' recover without fear. We travel by night from here on out."

It did not take long for sleep to take me.

✠

The hut was black as pitch and frightening. My dreams were near — red flames danced before my eyes. Though I'd not slept long, I was afraid to get back to it. Nearby, the Templar's soft and even breath hissed. I was glad that he could find rest.

Focus. Ground. Shield. Though I was not in the grip of a vision, the exercise helped push away my sudden fear. Beyond the hut I heard the whisper of the trees and the sound of the insects that chirped in the night. Still, I knew I'd feel better if I could but have a bit of light.

The Templar stirred and rolled over in his sleep. I was careful not to wake him and slowly began crawling toward the door. Straw was sharp beneath my palms. And as I put forward a knee, it came down hard on something. I barely muffled the cry.

Rooting around, my fingers curled around the hilt of a blade. I knew, even in the dark, that it was my dagger and that the Templar had left it for me. The one I had killed with. It felt different in my palm, heavier than I remembered. I closed my eyes, but opened them just as quickly when the memory followed me there. Overwhelmed, I stood and made my way outside.

The night was lit by a great number of stars. I sat on a rock by the door frame staring down at the dagger in my hand. The jewels in the hilt appeared dark without the light to shine on them. I thought they were very like me. I didn't feel as if the light shone on me, now that I was a killer. I did as the Templar had told me and said a prayer to the Almighty to help me bear this burden. I didn't feel any better when I had finished.

⊹

The Templar awoke shortly thereafter. I heard him moving about while I fed the horses the same oats that we had eaten earlier. When they finished, I watered them with two of the skins poured out into an old tin bucket I found by the side of the hut. I could hear his prayers now, a murmur that passed through the stone wall beside me.

As he finished, I went back inside to get my things. It was too dark to reckon, but I could see his bundles on the table and the staff with the blade inside. I carried them outside. While I waited, I unsheathed the blade from the staff and went through what I remembered of the exercises he had taught me. When he came outside, I resheathed it quickly.

"Keep that from here on out," he said. "I didn't like that ye had only the one dagger when it came down to a skirmish."

"Aye?" I said. "For my own?" I could not believe that he would trust me with something so amazing.

"Let us be gone from here. They will not be long away."

I tossed him a skin of water and the bag of oats. "Imagine them as toasted honey cakes," I said. "It seems to help."

He nodded and took them with little enthusiasm.

I fisted a handful of oats and chewed them dry. My imagination didn't work this time, and I could barely get them down. I wondered if I would ever get used to the sparse fare we were living on. My stomach felt like it touched my backbone.

The horses appeared well, even with the short rest we'd given them. They were strong, healthy animals, and I was appreciative of their service. We rode in silence for much of the night hours.

A SECRET REVEALED

As we came in sight of the hills that led to the peak of Montségur, the hair on my arms stood up despite the heat of the day. Up ahead I could see the dark line of the castle, stark against a crimson sky. With the sun going down beyond it, the castle seemed afire.

We made the road to the gates by nightfall, pushing our mounts as far as we might without harm. The castle was perched on the very top of a jut of stone, its walls apparently unchanged by time.

"We will sleep safely here," the Templar said. " 'Tis too far out o' the way for Philippe's men. The Hospitallers would not admit them. Within their walls no speech is allowed. Nor any outsiders. They will welcome us as brothers, but even if Philippe's men came an' insisted, they would not be admitted inside."

As we drew closer, the rise grew sharp, so we dismounted and walked the remaining distance to the main gate. The castle to me was a wonder. It was larger even than the Archbishop's residence and seemed completely impregnable.

A Hospitaller Brother met us at the gate, wariness in his eyes. The Templar exchanged a series of hand gestures that the Brother accepted, and we were led inside where we were relieved of our horses.

No one spoke as we were led to the main refectory for a meal with the rest of the knights. The head of their Order was in attendance, and so Templar Alexander sat at his side at the main table, while I sat below the dais at a long communal bench with the apprentices. I didn't mind. I was tired, and since no one was about to talk to me, I was able to sit, think, and eat. I was so relieved to be eating real food that it would not have mattered if I sat in a dung heap in the stables. A trencher of roast pheasant with heaping platters of vegetables filled me as I had not been filled in what felt like forever.

After the meal, we followed the knights and trainees to the main chapel for a silent Vespers prayer. It was good to feel part of a group such as this. They were like us, I thought. Like us. . . . This was the first time I had accepted readily that I was a part of the Templars. The thought pleased me.

Directly after prayers we were seen to our room. It was a sparse cell — two pallets with a tiny table between them — but it was very high up in the castle, and there was a window, though it had been shuttered to keep out any draft.

"Could we not open it a bit?" I asked. The room had been unused for a while, and it was stuffy from being closed. It had recently been dusted for our use and muskiness hung in the air.

"Aye. I don't see why not. I can just about reach." He strained upward and opened the window.

The night air was warm. "I bet ye can see forever from here," I said. "Would it be all right if I looked out?"

"Aye," he said, helping me drag the small table over beneath the window. "But be careful."

The view when I gained the table was wondrous. Outside, far below, the land sloped sharply. Rocks and scrub dotted a swath of deep green that stretched for miles. It was beautiful.

I turned back to descibe it for him, but didn't get that far. The carving began to glow at my waist, and I felt myself waver on the table.

Dark figures crouched by the window. A light bag passed hand to hand, then was tied to a waist. Moonlight illuminated a man. The view down from a staggering height made me reel.

The table tilted beneath my feet, and I felt myself falling.

"Tormod!"

The Templar caught me as I toppled to the floor. "Monks," I said, gasping. "Four escaped with something in a sack. There was fighting beyond."

"What was in the sack? Can ye describe it?"

"Small, about the size o' two o' my fists. 'Twas important." I met his eyes. "They were desperate to remove it before this castle fell."

He was quiet, thinking. "There is a legend that surrounds this place," he said. "Monks escaped during a siege o' this castle. 'Tis said they went down the wall with something worth dying for."

I stared out the window, thinking on what I'd seen.

We left after Lauds, greeting the rise of the sun with the Hospitallers in residence. Our horses were refreshed, well fed and watered. We were renewed as well. The head of the Order saw us to the gates and outside the castle. Only then did he speak.

"Your letters o' transport," he said, handing over a small scroll that the Templar tucked in his sporran. I knew from an earlier conversation that there were trade agreements long in place between the houses of Hospitaller and Templar. It was a form of checks and balances. The Templar had gone off earlier and signed a contract with the house. They provided us with coin and this letter of transport, which was passage for two aboard a Hospitaller ship, docked in the harbor down the coast. They would, in turn, receive payment from our house, the Templars, when next their transactions were due.

"Thank ye, Brother," said the Templar. "We are forever grateful o' yer hospitality."

He nodded and went back inside. As we rode away, I asked, "Do they do that for others? Lend money? Make travel arrangements?"

"Aye. The Templars originated the process. When a man goes on pilgrimage, instead o' risking his currency to brigands, he is able to deposit his gold with the preceptory closest his home. He receives from the preceptory a coded chit that he then can redeem on the opposite shore for his currency, minus the fare for his passage."

I thought it a brilliant scheme.

When we reached level land, I looked back on the castle, remembering the vision of the monks who had gone out the window and down the steep mountainside. The weight of the carving in my sporran seemed to multiply.

BY LAND OR SEA

We boarded the Hospitaller ship as the sun sank in the golden sky two days later. The ship lay at anchor in the harbor of the village of Perpignan and was set to sail before nightfall for Avignon, still several days away. The Templar went below to rest. Travel had been hard on him. He slept far less than I did, and now, secure for the moment, he gave in to the need.

I, however, could not stand being stuck inside the ship after so long living on the land. The crush of people belowdecks was intrusive, and my mind was still much occupied with thoughts of those hunting us.

I went up on deck, pleased at the way my body so quickly adjusted to the sway. I wandered, trying to stay out of the way of the men preparing for the ship's departure. It was strange not to have any duties, when the last time I'd sailed I'd had so many.

I watched the crewmen scramble up and down the ridgepole of the main mast like Seamus had done. Though I would never have credited it, I was a bit melancholy about his capture. The thought made me smile — when had I ever mourned the loss of Seamus's company?

But so much had happened. So much had changed. The petty squabbles we had didn't seem to bear much weight now.

I thought of my brother Torquil. The trivial wrongs that we fought over were even less important than the ones with Seamus. If I ever got a chance, I decided that I would make it up to him.

The wind swept the deck and the sails towering above billowed. A group of gulls flew and hovered looking for scraps of refuse that the sailors would occasionally dump over the side. Their cry split the air, and I squinted to see the sailors above as they moved with ease from one handhold to the next, tightening the ropes and checking the lines for frays.

"You, boy. Get above and check the sails from the crow's nest."

He had mistaken me for one of them, perhaps because I had changed out of my pilgrim garb into my old breeks, tunic, and boots. But I didn't hesitate. I approached the ridgepole and started up. It was not a difficult climb, but the winds were high and the ship was dipping ferociously in the waves. Several times I had to stop and readjust my foot. Without the missing toes, and with the loose boot, I had to compensate by squeezing my muscles and clenching my foot. Slowly I ascended and came in sight of the basket that surrounded the main mast. No wonder the man had sent me. It was small. And it was not nearly as solid and secure as I had anticipated. The platform of wicker, woven to an inner and outer steel frame, had steep sides, but was open in a space about as wide as I was across the chest. There were holes in the base, and more in the sides, so I carefully made my way around the weak bits, seeking the stronger, safer parts.

Far down below, the ocean rolled, glistening beneath the golden rays of the evening sun. Away, off in the distance lay only the vast ocean, and yet, staring back from whence we'd come, I saw the beauty of the mountains. I was entranced by the play of light across their crystal peaks.

Lathered horses pounded across a green field. Blue-and-gold banners snapped in the wind.

I came to with a force that made me reel and my foot slipped through one of the gaps in the wicker. I screamed, teetering back.

A COMING DANGER

I threw my arms wide and with a shock connected with the upper rib of the basket. Pain shot through me. My shoulder felt ripped from my body. Sweat pooled beneath my fingers. High above the ocean, I hung.

Cries of alarm came from below as a crowd gathered. "Go easy, lad. Hold tight. Help is coming."

It won't be soon enough. Fear was so close and tight in my chest I was sure I would faint. I swung my legs to the lower rim. They didn't connect. Desperate, I grabbed the ridgepole between my legs and clung with all my might. The ocean yawned far below. I felt the pull of it, as if I were being dragged downward. My arms and legs were trembling. I cast my mind out and away, seeking help. The wind was blowing mildly. Frantic, I tried to whisper it into shape. Then, suddenly, the carving flared with heat below my waist. With the heat came the wind, and I was able to move my legs up the mast feeling buffered, lifted by a strong and sudden gale.

Higher. Higher. Then just a bit more. At last, I felt the metal of the bottom rung beneath my legs. With near disbelief and a last burst of energy I leaned back and hoisted myself once more to safety.

The wind dropped off as suddenly as it had risen. Gulls swooped in arcs above. I shook so badly that I dared not move. When the first of the sailors reached my perch, it took me a moment to realize he was there.

"Boy. Give me your hand," he said. His eyes were blue, deep as the sky, and kind. It's strange that I should notice such things when I had very nearly dropped to my death, but there it is. I took his hand in mine and let him pull me upright.

"Good. Just come toward me and I'll see you down." He had me scoot back from the hole and turn so that my body faced the pole and my feet were squarely on the rungs. He was at my back with his legs spread wide to a second set of holds. "Now, easy as a babe's first steps, we'll just go down this together."

And we did. In no time at all I was once again on deck. My body was a mass of aches. The Templar was waiting.

"Is there ever a time when I'll not have to worry over

ye, Tormod?" His anger was justified but I had no mind for it.

"They're coming," I said. "We have to get off the ship."

His head jerked toward shore. "Quickly, go below. Get our things. We must be off before they sail."

I scrambled to do as he bid. We didn't have much. I took the staff, and the water skins, the bags of oats, my plaid, and the bundle of tied-up supplies that was his. The horses had already been boarded, and we could not wait to have them brought up; they would have to stay.

I met him on deck bare moments later, where he paid for a coracle that would take us ashore. We boarded as fast as we could. As the Templar rowed, the dread in my chest grew. We didn't wait until it was fully beached before we were out and running. We left the coracle bobbing in the wash.

The sand gave way beneath my feet. The loss of toes made my gait less smooth. We made it to the trees, breathing hard. I felt them. The carving was afire. They were close.

FROM BEYOND THE TREES

Just as I thought that maybe we were mistaken, I saw them. With banner unfurled, the first of the men broke through the far clump of trees. Following in his wake were the rest: a group of eight men, armed, and in full fighting force. They wheeled up on the shore watching the ship leave.

I held my breath as they regrouped and spoke to one another. Then, as one, they turned back the way they'd come. My heart beat a frantic tattoo.

"Come, before they realize we are not aboard," he said. "Hurry, Tormod, an' don't speak."

We moved, into and out of the shadows, silent and wary. There was no place safe. I knew it for truth.

Skirting the wood's edge, we paced the shore. The heat was high and the midges were thick. We followed no path but stepped over rocks and downed trees, making our way ever north. We came often to a place that was impassable and, when this happened, backtracked until we were clear.

I felt like my bones were strung on a harp. I imagined

the hunters around every bush and tree, and their eyes on me at each turn.

The Templar had sunk into himself, leaving me with only my terrified thoughts for company.

It was late in the night when we came to the wood's end, several leagues up the coast. I assumed that we would continue on across the road and into the field ahead, and so I nearly shrieked when the Templar put out his hand to stop my progress.

"Go softly here," he said quietly. "Just ahead is a safe house, a kirk where we will be among friends. Speak nothing o' our business, even if it appears all right to do so."

I nodded.

The kirk was a small stone hut set amid a tumble of bushes and trees. It didn't look at all like a kirk to me. It had no cross, no sacred well, nothing that marked it as a place of worship. Only the barest of paths led to it. I could see no light inside, not from beneath or around the door frame.

"I don't think anyone is a' home," I whispered.

"Hush," he said. "Not another word until I tell ye 'tis safe." The Templar was more wary than I'd ever seen him. He scanned the area and seemed to hesitate, something he had never in all our travels done. I would have spoken to him about it, but his hushed warning, and the fact that I always seemed to do the wrong thing in these situations, stilled my tongue.

On his signal, we set out across the clearing, crouching low and making little noise. He stood outside — stock-still, listening. It was then I thought of the carving. I had turned my sporran to the back, and it was buried beneath my plaid.

The Templar was still waiting to make up his mind, and I shifted the plaid and made to turn the whole thing around just as he knocked on the door. I could not see it, but suddenly I could feel its heat flaring.

BETRAYAL

The door of the kirk opened inward. It was difficult to see inside. Only the sullen glow of a small fire lit the gloom. As we passed beyond the frame, I kept close to the Templar, nearly treading on his heels.

I knew even before the door shut behind us that we had made a grave error in coming here. The carving at my back was burning. The Templar realized his mistake at the same time, for he shoved me back that he might draw his sword. A scratch of flint, then flare of light

filled the dark before us as a rush torch suddenly flickered to life.

My heart dropped, and I drew a ragged breath. We
were surrounded. Six or seven soldiers in the colors of
blue and gold crowded the room, their swords drawn.
There was nowhere to turn.

One of the soldiers dragged a man forward. His
clothes were in tatters, his face badly bruised and swollen. He was barely able to stand. "Is this the man?"
demanded the soldier, giving his ward a shake that made
the man's hood slide back from his head.

I sucked in a breath, sick in my heart and soul. *No!
It cannot be.*

"Is it? Answer me or you will not live to see the
morning," he shouted, prodding the man with the hilt of
his sword.

Seamus's head rolled back. I could see the spittle
slide down his chin. "Aye," he whispered. "God save
him, it is."

Betrayal.

I was mortified, but that was nothing compared to
the emotion ripping through the Templar. I sensed the
jump in tension and grabbed his sword arm, holding on
tight.

"Alexander Sinclair, you are under arrest for the
crimes of heresy and treason. As mandated by King
Philippe of France, you are to lay down your sword."

I could almost see his mind calculating the odds of taking on every man in the room. In the end it was Seamus who decided him.

"Stop it, Alex. They will kill us all." His words were a whisper filled with the fear of knowledge. He knew what they were capable of; he had been in their hands for a long while.

With great effort, the Templar lowered his sword.

What filled me most with fear was the possible discovery of the carving. All I could think of was his vision, of the broken carving and the world falling into ruin. I tried not to draw attention to myself.

One of the soldiers looked my way nonetheless. *He is o' no consequence.* The Templar's push was as light as air. *Just an underling. Not worth yer notice.* The man's eyes moved on, dismissing me. I took a quick breath, shaken.

The Templar submitted without argument. I did the same.

Rough hands turned us about and quickly we were bound. The sharp cut of the frayed rope chafed my skin. I tried to make a fist with one hand so that later I might be able to slip the bonds, but the large hairy soldier who tied me thought my efforts a joke. He yanked the ropes even tighter, and I cried out. I could not feel my hands and my wrists burned like fire.

My captor jerked me forward by my ropes, and I

bit the inside of my cheek to keep back the scream. They dragged us outside. Though we didn't struggle, they seemed pleased to do whatever harm they might. I supposed that they must have been hunting us long.

Horses were brought from behind a hut across the field. They had taken no chances. The Templar spoke not at all, but when his eyes met mine, his impressions seemed to echo inside my head. *Safeguard it.*

A CHANCE

What I recall of the road was a long and grueling trek with none of the pleasantry that I'd shared with the Templar. The soldiers treated us as the criminals we were branded. Food came in the form of a hunk of moldy bread that I had to pick the weevils out of with my teeth. Drink was the last dregs of a watered wine that tasted sour and made my stomach heave. And yet it came infrequently, so I took and ate every bit that was offered. We stopped only twice during the days, when the soldiers needed to void. We were allowed to go at the same time, but it was difficult in that our hands were still bound before us. And they stood watch all the while.

They didn't pay me as much heed as they did the Templar. I was of no concern. I was just a boy. They had not searched my body and found the carving. His whisper had worked. For once being considered nothing played out in my favor. I listened to their words at night; I knew that they were frightened of him. A caged and cornered Templar was something to fear. We all knew the stories telling of the oath that in battle a Templar would never give up; he would fight unto death. Watching him, from my place, tied to the tree opposite, I knew that he was working it in his mind, looking for the opportunity, seeking the moment they would make a mistake.

We were a week into the travel, moving north and west by my calculation of the sun and the stars. The roads were harsh and untraveled, and my mind remained frozen and filled with fear. Seamus was tied to the horse that held the supplies. He was in rough shape. I could see the welts on his back, for the blood had seeped through his tunic.

I had branded him traitor, and yet what information they took from him was at a cost that, in all truth, I didn't think I, in his place, would not too have paid. He swayed in the saddle, and several times he fainted away completely. The soldiers treated him roughly when he slipped, twice, sideways. That was when they had tied him, with his face to the horse's mane, spread-eagle, his arms and legs tied round the animal's neck and girth.

The Templar watched him with worried eyes. I did as well. I didn't like Seamus, especially in light of my injury and the fact that he had led these men to us, but I didn't think either act was something he should die for.

Thoughts of the carving kept me on edge. At all costs it had to remain hidden, but this was proving difficult. The blaze of its heat flared beneath my plaid in the sporran at the base of my spine. What was it trying to tell me? The danger was already upon us. My thoughts drifted. I was hot and tired. My bonds were too tight. The skin beneath was raw and bleeding.

We were not allowed to speak to each other, but they could not in truth quiet us from saying our prayers unless they gagged us. It was not above them, but they didn't do it. And so each time I heard his soft murmur, as I did now, I added my voice just as quietly. This time the feel of a rise in the power floating on the air while we prayed surprised me.

I tried to look, without seeming to, over at the Templar. His eyes were turned in my direction, and yet even from where I sat I could tell he was in the trancelike state of the vision sense. I heard him then.

His voice was soft, playing at the very edges of my hearing. Though his prayers continued, and all there could hear him plainly, I could hear something else as well. I could hear him speak only to me.

Remember the ledge. Seek the life. Rope once a plant.

I thought to answer him, but he knew and forestalled me. *Don't speak.*

It was difficult to keep silent, but I held my tongue and concentrated on fraying the rope. The challenge was unique, different than feeling the sap running through the trees. The rope was something long dead. I had to reach far, and think on the hemp that was, to find even a whisper of its former life. But when I did, it was so clear that I wanted to shout for joy. I very nearly lost my place in the prayer but caught myself in time.

I could see and feel the inner life of the ropes, and I knew that I was doing just as the Templar asked. *Hold now,* he whispered.

As the prayer ended, I let the link I felt with the rope seep into the earth's memory, back from where it had come. The Templar's head rested on his chest. I had no doubt that holding the link with me while he worked on his ropes had been draining.

I was frightened. I didn't want to look at any of the guards, but I could not help myself. The closest one met my eyes, and I felt a hard slap from his hand. My head snapped back. I flinched with the shock of the pain. And yet, I would rather that reaction than the one he would have shown if he had noticed anything had transpired.

Night. I didn't know whether I wished it would arrive sooner or later.

⊹

The dark settled in around us. Sounds of the night filled the air. Most of the guards lay sleeping scattered around the perimeter, their weapons at their sides.

My hands were cold. I could feel nothing of the tips. It was as if they were dead. Gone, like my toes. It was a terrifying thought. I sat up straighter, pressing my back against the tree, feeling the bite of the bark and peering down through the dark toward my bound wrists. Memories filled my mind, dark whispers of waking to the pain and horror of my mangled foot. A small, frightened whimper escaped my mouth, and in a panic I yanked at my bonds.

And then, suddenly, I was free.

I sat for a moment of disbelief, trying to steady my breathing. I was thankful then of the dark, for it hid my face as feeling rushed into my hands, like a fire raging through my arms and on down my wrists. I was near to shrieking with it.

Easy, he whispered into my mind.

I looked across the way to where the Templar was tied. I could see nothing but the vague shape of him in the dark. *Seamus?*

The first time I tried to speak back felt as if my mind was coated in a thick layer of sheep's wool — my thoughts, my words had to fight their way past. *No movement.*

Staff?

Aye. One of the men had taken it from me when they arrested us.

My sword?

On your horse. It was slowly getting easier to form the words.

Take Seamus. Escape.

His words sent a chill up my spine. I thought for a long while about the moves he had taught me, and the conflict about to come. But no matter how much I thought on it, when it happened, I was not nearly as prepared as I had hoped.

The clearing was dark and quiet, save for the crickets chirping all around. My hands had long since regained their feeling; now they just shook with terror. I stayed awake, watching the moon, watching the Templar, waiting.

And then I heard him again.

Now. Ride. Don't look back.

I wanted to protest, but I knew it would do no good. He meant for us to escape, and he was going to do everything he could to make it happen.

I turned my knees to the side, and started up. It felt as if the noise I made was enough to wake the dead, but no one noticed. Crouching low, I slowly began edging my way from the cover of the tree.

The moon was high, but its light didn't shine on me. I was mindful to move as he had taught me, softly, without disturbing the ground cover. Twigs and rocks were thick beneath my feet, but I traveled over them with barely a whisper of sound.

My heart pounded so strongly I thought I would die long before I reached Seamus. But then scarcely before I could credit it, I was there. Quickly, I stooped to feel his chest. He moaned as I turned him from his side to his back and didn't open his eyes at all. "Shhh," I said.

They had not bothered to tie his hands. I could see why. He was burning with fever and was no real worry to them. So they thought, anyway. I was hoping to prove them wrong. Stepping past Seamus, I reached for the Templar's staff, which lay on the ground nearby. The men didn't hear, but the horses did.

They began to balk and shy, their ears pressed forward. I was terrified they would give me away, and without thinking, I spoke, the same way I had to the

Templar, reaching for the mind of his horse first. The mount was all impulse and feelings.

Hush ye now, laddie. I combined my words with thoughts of safety and peace, and he and the next quieted. I was pleased with the accomplishment.

In the clearing something was happening. I saw the shadow of the Templar rise. I held my breath, waiting. It seemed as if the night stopped: The crickets went silent, and the wind paused with me.

"Non nobis, Domine!" His war cry brought the guard and those who slept rushing across the clearing. He was unarmed, but in the moment it took for me to spy him out, he had already taken the sword from the nearest.

Wasting not a moment, I sprang to my feet and loosed the horses' reins. Swiping the nearest across the hindquarters, I mentally shouted *Go!* The horse took off, bolting straight through the camp toward the Templar and the men fighting him.

I didn't stop to watch further, but did as he'd instructed me. I took the next horse, his own, to Seamus's side, hauled the man to a sitting position, and tried to get him to stand.

He was heavy, more than I expected. I could barely move him. *Please, Seamus. Help,* I begged, sending the words directly into his sleeping brain. For a moment nothing happened but then, somehow, he seemed to hear. With a moan he came back to me.

"Hurry, Seamus. Just help me get ye into the saddle. Please, we have to get out o' here." The swordplay was loud behind us. I didn't know how many the Templar had engaged, but it was too much to hope that their attention would only be on him. Near me a soldier shouted. My breath came in gasps. "Now, Seamus, now." I put the whole of my strength into lifting him up over my shoulder. I know that he helped, though it didn't seem to be much or enough, but somehow I flung him over the saddle. He pulled himself forward using our bags as leverage, and at last lay sprawled along on the horse's neck. The mount jostled, forward and back, not sure of the weight that was suddenly on him.

I took the momentary boon to draw the slender sword from the sheath of the staff. It was a good thing I did.

Like images frozen in time, the memories of my training came back to me. Balanced with sheath in one hand and sword in the other I waited for the soldier that came on attack. It could only have been a moment, but it was as if everything stilled just so that I could equip myself. And then it started.

I swung my blade, bracing for the heaviness of the soldier's sword as it encountered my own. Then, changing balance, I countered and spun out of his way. His went wide and missed me, and I slipped past his guard.

My blade drew blood, cutting strongly through his clothing.

Infuriated, he hacked down from above. I sprang to my right, leaving him grappling with air. It was then that I saw the opening. As if we were sparring on the ship, I felt the deep knowledge that the next stroke would be mine. Without pause I took it, swiping my blade cleanly across his neck.

Exhilaration turned to horror as I watched the stripe of red well and gape. The bile rose in me, and I turned, blind, back to Seamus. The horse had been standing idle, shifting, trying to decide what it was supposed to do. My hands were on the saddle before I could think. Then from nowhere, I heard the Templar's voice in my head. *Go. Now!*

I sheathed the blade, tucked it under my arm, and vaulted into the saddle behind Seamus, nearly bringing us both down. With a great heave, I leaned onto Seamus, grasped the reins, and shouted like a man gone mad. "Go, go, go!"

RIDE LIKE THE WIND

The horse bolted just in time, plowing directly into the path of a soldier rushing us. I kicked out with my leg and caught the man in the chest, knocking him back and away. Then I tucked my legs tight to the horse's sides and mentally shouted to run like the wind.

He did. Past the clearing and out of the woods. There was nothing before us but hills and vales.

I was desperate to know how the Templar was faring, but I knew that I would do just as he said, get away and take the carving with me. I felt it then, as if the mere thought called it to life. Its burn scalded clear through the sporran, still tucked beneath my robe.

We rode like demons were on our tail, never looking back, never slowing, cutting east, then north, to make the trail difficult to follow. We slowed when I was sure no one was behind. Then, and only then, did I think about what had happened and what I had done.

This was not the first time I had killed, and I thought it should have been easier to bear. But it was not. I could not fool myself into believing I had acted on impulse.

That was a part of it, but I knew full well that, in the heat of the fight, I was in it all the way. It was kill or be killed, and somehow, right now, that seemed even worse.

I slid from the horse, careful not to take Seamus with me, and walked beside. The night air was cool on my hot skin. The sounds of nature loud. I heard the call of a wolf in the distance. A sennight ago it would have frightened me greatly, yet now, I could barely rouse myself to feel anything but the guilt and remorse filling my soul.

I led the horse deep into a copse. Morning was drawing near. I didn't deceive myself into thinking they would not come after us, but hoped and prayed that the Templar would find us first.

With as many soft fronds as I could gather, I made a pallet for Seamus. When it was right, I dragged him from the horse and laid him on it. His color was not encouraging: white like the lime we washed the great boulder with in the square at home so very long ago. Enormous dark circles ringed his eyes, and his cheeks were sunken and sallow.

I washed his face with water from the skin and checked the wounds on his body. The whippings he had endured left horrific marks I could never have imagined if I'd not seen them. His skin was purely stripped away in many places, and I could see beyond to the inside of him. I thought that the damage would make me sick, but oddly it didn't.

I had no salve like the one Brother Bertrand had used, but I did my best to clean the wounds as he had done, hoping that would help. My body was fit to drop when finally I finished. With everything in me I tried to stay awake, waiting for the Templar to come. He'd feel my soul's signature, I knew, as he had done from the beginning, and he would find us.

I fell asleep beside Seamus, with the horse tied to a nearby branch. It was not until I was deeply asleep that I had the vision that showed how very wrong I had been.

ALONE

A sword glinted in the moonlight, sweeping a path of destruction. Men were swarming. More than he could handle.

I woke shaking, terrified. He was not coming. He had not gotten away. Seamus was no help to me, and the Templar was somewhere, captured and beaten at the very least. I had to do something, but what?

I looked over at Seamus, so still, so frighteningly deathlike. I felt the slow, steady beat of the land beneath us. The carving was warm — not the glowing, burning fire of danger, but a steady, solid presence. I turned the sporran to the front and took the carving in my hand.

Its glow was heartening. As beaten down and discouraged as I was, the carving gave me hope. And it gave me something else. Suddenly I had a strange compulsion to lay my hands on Seamus. With nothing left to lose, I set the carving on his chest and rested my hands beside it.

Tingling heat ran through my fingers, and I felt myself drift, welcoming my other sense.

I saw deep into Seamus — beneath his skin to the very essence of bone and muscle. And without any doubt whatsoever, I knew how to make him whole once again and set about it.

Sweat rose on my skin and exhaustion weighted my limbs. What I was doing was taking its own toll on my body, but I continued knitting ripped and torn muscle, feeding blood to the places that were in need, healing the bones, speeding his body on its way to recovery.

As the sun set once again in the hot sky, I came to, lying half on, half off Seamus's chest, with the carving nestled safely in my hands.

"Get off, Tormod," I heard his weak voice say. "Ye're crushing me."

"Ye took yer time about waking," I said, rolling exhausted to his side. I slept then for so many marks of the candle I cannot even reckon them.

CONTRITION

I woke reaching for the carving, rooting around behind and under me. I was in a panic until I felt it pressing into my thigh beneath the fold of my robe.

"Here," Seamus said. "Eat."

He had foraged and found a variety of nuts and wild mushrooms. "Not much in the way o' a feast, but it fills the emptiness."

"Water?" I asked, groggily.

"Aye. Here." He handed me a skin, and I drank until I needed to come up for air.

"Ye healed me." Wonder filled his voice, but I sensed as well something was not as it should be. "Why did ye do it? Why did ye not let me die, as I should have?"

There was a darkness to him, a bleak despair that I felt coming off him in waves. As I was aware of the land, I now was aware of Seamus. Something in me had changed.

"No one should die when they are not destined to," I said. "'Tis a sin to wish it on yerself."

His eyes turned to me. "I have betrayed him an' given us all over to death. I wish mine to come now."

"No. Speak not that way," I said. "The Templar is in need. Somehow we must work together to help him."

I looked to the night sky where a bright star to the north pointed the direction we would travel to follow the map, but we would not follow it as yet.

"How long did I sleep?" I was worried. The vision of the Templar's fight for our lives hung sharply in my mind's eye.

"A night an' a day. I tried to wake ye, but it was to no avail." There was a listlessness to Seamus that worried me.

"Tell me what has happened to ye, and I will do the same," I said. "'Tis only with the full truth between us that we might hope to salvage this day."

He spoke of the night we disappeared. "They boarded the ship no' more than a candle mark after ye'd left. Not soldiers, but mercenaries. They had orders to keep us alive an' deliver us to Philippe." He spoke the tale without passion, as if it were nothing to him.

"We were taken to Paris for questioning." He shivered, and I noticed that he could not seem to stop. He clamped his hands together to try and still them. His face was white, and I could feel the fear and revulsion projecting from his mind.

"I gave them everything. All they could want an' more. I will pay for it with the price o' my soul." His head was low. Nothing I could say would have made a difference. I kept silent, feeling the press of his emotions beneath the surface of his mind.

"What did ye tell them, Seamus?"

"That Alex is following a map, seeking whatever lies a' its end." He took a short breath. "They know his safe places an' that the stars are the markers. They know he has a talisman that is helping him find his way."

My breath came out in a rush. "Ye gave him away! How could ye?"

"Do ye think for a moment that I don't ask myself that? Ye've no idea what Philippe is like, Tormod. So fair an' fine-looking, but he has the soul of a viper. The things that he did, the tortures he devised . . ." Beads of sweat gathered on his forehead. "An' now they have Alexander an' the carving. 'Tis over."

The bulk of the carving felt heavy in my sporran. Should I tell Seamus that Philippe's men did not have it? Should I give the carving over to him? Had he not already compromised our duty? Would he do it again?

The Templar's words echoed in my mind. *Trust no one. Safeguard it.*

A wash of fear crested in me. Would not these same tortures befall the Templar if he had survived the last encounter?

"We must go back," I said.

Seamus looked at me long and hard. I saw something flash in the depths of his eyes, and it frightened me. It was a longing, a longing for death.

PART THREE

RETURN

We took the chance that it was the last thing they would ever expect — that we would return. Seamus and I back-tracked to the place we had been. The ash of the fire was long cold, but Seamus knew where they were going. He had been in and out of consciousness for many days before they found us, and had listened when they thought that he could not.

They were taking him to the walled city of Carcassonne, no more than a day from our last camp. Philippe waited there for word from his men on the ambush set for us.

We rode as fast as our burdened mount would take us, stopping only long enough to dismount and walk for stretches to relieve him. The land was easy. Slight slopes and valleys filled much of the trek, then gave way to a heavily forested wood. The wind was brisk. A seasonal storm was setting to open up on us. The skies were dark and overcast, and the hills a myriad of summer green.

My mind twisted and turned, thoughts whirling without beginning or end, all centered on how we could do anything to aid the Templar. He would be heavily guarded. And we were but two.

For all my thinking, I had come up with nothing by the time we arrived, and a feeling of despair settled over me. The city was a fortress. Its walls were great blocks of granite. Its windows were few and set high in the towers. Guards patrolled the gate, and sentries stood in the towers. How would we ever get inside, and what would we do then?

We camped in the woods, watching and timing the guards. I repeated the rotation aloud often in that first day, marking time with the progression of the sun across the sky. Seamus sat and watched silently. Where his mind had gone I had no idea, but late on the second day of our watch he spoke.

"There's got to be a way in."

I saw it just when he did. A single horse-drawn cart traveled the path to the gates.

We waited several candle marks. Time seemed to stretch on forever. Finally the cart reappeared, and it was no longer empty.

"Stay here," Seamus said. "I'll be back shortly. If anyone marks me, I rely on ye to cover my back."

He left me standing there wondering just how I was supposed to do that. I drew my dagger and crouched in the tree cover, the sword from the staff at my side. The wind blew down over the valley, rustling the branches, rattling my knees. Every noise made me jump. Every breath I took was labored.

Seamus appeared driving the wagon a short while later. Where the former driver and his passenger were, I didn't know, but he now wore a dull brown robe over his tunic. "Get in and pull yer hat low."

I climbed up and glanced back into the wagon. Fresh dark splotches stained the wooden planking.

He pulled the cart off to the side of the road. Waiting. Watching. I wanted to ask him what we were doing, but he had the look of the Templar — absolute concentration. A quarter mark of the candle later, he urged the wagon back onto the road.

"The new guards are in place. Let us hope they didn't speak much on the change." He flicked the reins. "Keep yer head down an' say nothing." I'd never seen him this way — solid, serious, deadly. I ducked my head and we rolled on across the drawbridge and boldly up to the gate.

"State yer business," called the guard.

"We're to pick up a body. Overdue, too," he added.

"You were supposed to be here earlier," the man said keenly.

My heart was beating triple time. Without thought I called up the power of the land and whispered a push of uncertainty. Immediately I felt the hum of another. Seamus had added his influence. The guard did not pause, just called for the gate to open, and the cart rolled inside with no fanfare.

Inside was a wide cobbled road. Seamus urged the horse with the reins and slowly we clopped up the slope, around the bend, and out of the sight of the guards.

"Ye've learned something while we were apart," said Seamus. This was as close to a compliment as ever I had received from him.

In a dark alleyway, in a seemingly less used part of the city, we tied up the horse and wagon and set out on foot. "They've got to have him in the citadel. They spoke o' cells in the bowels o' the city, where the inquisitor has free rein."

The thought made me move faster. I had been lagging, frightened by the silence around me and over the ease of our entrance. With barely a sound we slipped through the darkened alleys. Seamus moved with unerring accuracy. "How do ye know where ye're going?" I whispered.

"There is only one way, Tormod," he said. "Can ye no' feel his pain?"

I glanced quickly at Seamus. His face was pale.

I focused and found that I could feel the trace of the Templar's aura, mingling with the beat of the land. Pain rippled across the surface of my back. I hissed, wishing that I hadn't.

"Distance yerself," he commanded. I heard him but was too caught up in what I had tapped. "Focus. Ground. Shield!" he snapped. He sounded so like the Templar that I reacted and the pain receded. "Good. Ye need to practice that, Tormod. Ye cannot allow yerself to get trapped in a loop o' someone else's aura. Ye might never regain yer full faculties."

This Seamus was new to me. I didn't know what to say. I followed him without a word through the alleys and around corners as he tracked the Templar's pain. I did not, however, open myself to that trail again. Seamus led the way.

The citadel was a heavily protected keep built into the rock of the hillside in the lowest part of the city. Two guards stood at the front and one patrolled the roof. We crept around the perimeter looking for an entrance, but there was no other way in.

"No one goes in or out," Seamus murmured. "The guards are on high alert." I was stooped next to him beside the eastern wall of the keep. The ground beneath my feet was soft and smelled badly. I moved to Seamus's left to seek stronger purchase.

"God's thumbs, Tormod. What did ye step in?" He shook his head to clear the smell from his nose.

"I don't know, but it's making my eyes tear. Seems to be a stream o' it running right through here." I scraped my boots on the harder dirt trying to get rid of the filth. Then it hit me. "No one goes in, but something is getting out. Look!" It was hard to see in the dark when not seeking it, but once recognized, it was discernible. The stream of muck was leaching from a grate set low in the side of the keep. A gulley of runoff snaked directly to where I'd been standing. The privy pits.

THE  PRIVY PITS

"Do ye think we could fit through?" I asked staring at the grate and dark space behind.

"Aye. It looks to be wide enough for two side by side, but 'tis only waist high. I don't know what's on the other side o' it, but 'tis worth a try, don't ye think?" A rotten smell wafted up my nose. It was all I could do to keep from answering no. This foul, disgusting discovery had been mine.

"Let's go," I said, anxious to be on our way.

"Hold," said Seamus. "If I've not offended the Lord, mayhap He will help us in our endeavor." He made the sign of the cross and I followed. "Our Father, who art in heaven . . ."

We clasped arms, as I'd seen him do with the Templar. "May the Lord guide our steps," he said.

"And our faith remain true," I replied. Seamus could not seem to meet my gaze, and I wondered for a moment what was wrong.

I didn't, however, have time to think on it, for it was time to move. The guards were leaving their post to brief the sentries coming on duty. We would only have moments, and we took the opportunity given, leaving our concealment at a sprint. We followed the path of the foul-smelling stream across the way and up to the wall. To avoid their eyes, we flattened ourselves against it and inched our way to the grate. Seamus leapt the small mouth of the gulley and positioned himself on one side. I stayed on the other. Then, as one, we met in the middle and tested its strength.

On the first tug it moved not at all, but on the second there was a wavering, and the mortar used to hold it in place crumbled beneath our onslaught. The grate was very old, and the constant flow of muck had eroded its metal edges. I could hear the guards moving into place. They were not directly above, but close enough that I thought I'd die then and there.

On the third try the grate came free with a soft rusted whine. Quickly we threw ourselves back, flat against the wall. I heard the guards approach, above.

Pressure blossomed in the back of my eyes, and I felt the hum coming from Seamus.

"Just a boar," said a guard.

"A nice meal that would make, eh?" spoke another.

"A sight better than the stale oats we've been given," replied the first.

The sound of their footsteps receding allowed me to breathe once again. Seamus motioned me in. With one last breath of somewhat fresh air, I ducked and darted in through the grate.

Ugh! It was all I could do not to shout the word aloud. The place was disgusting, as foul as ever I had smelled. In the black of the pits was the refuse of many. As we stepped into the depth of it, the slime slid past my ankles. I felt it squish beneath my boots, and when I forced myself to put my hands before me, I touched a wall that was coated.

"Gawd," I whispered, snatching my fingers back. I was at the base of a long shaft. The space was actually quite wide at the bottom. Seamus entered a moment later and I heard a slight gagging as he fought to keep from retching.

I had moved as far as the hole would allow me, to the left. Now, I hurried past him, to the right. Ahead there was a door. On it a small, rusted latch snapped off at my touch, leaving us locked out where we were.

"Great." Seamus's disgust was near on as annoying as it had been on the ship.

"Well, if ye've got a better way," I snapped.

"Shhh." He hissed. "Step back."

Inside the corridor a disturbing sound reverberated, a strange rustle and crack that chilled me to the bone. Beside me Seamus gagged.

"What?" I whispered.

"Cat-o'-nine." His voice was strangled. "The lash."

My body went cold as the sound came with an unrelenting rhythm. Without wanting to, I strained to hear the gasp of a prayer between the lash strokes.

In my mind I matched his prayers, sick in my heart and soul. Questions fell but none were answered. The lashing seemed as if it would go on an eternity.

"Back." Seamus's sudden whisper had me scrambling away from him. A soft thrum seemed to fill the space around us as he laid his hands on the door. It was black as pitch, but the edges of him faintly glowed. His body was stiff and still. Then from beyond the door the lashing and questions stopped. The door to a cell opened, and the sound of men passing came to me.

We waited in silence. I would not make the mistakes I had made with the Templar. Seamus moved first. "Give me yer dagger."

I fished it from my sporran and handed it to him.

He jammed it hard in the latch I had broken. It seemed impossible that it worked and no one heard, but moments later the door opened.

The light from a torch slowly filled the space, then waned as whoever had been there disappeared on their way.

"Others will not be far off. They'd not leave him alone." His voice was low and breathless. Slowly we crept out. The corridor bent a short distance away, and he held me back.

"Stay here a moment." I didn't even hear his steps, but a moment later came a dull thud, the sound of something large hitting the floor. In the dark silence I heard the soft rattle of keys.

"Tormod, come," he whispered loudly.

I moved quickly, stumbling, but righting myself when my feet encountered a body on the floor. "Is he dead?" I asked, sickened.

"No. Come, help me."

✠

The Templar was unconscious, his breathing shallow, and he moaned when we rolled him onto his back. His face was bleeding. I grew nauseous at the warm feel of his blood beneath my fingers. The vestment on his back was shredded.

"What have they done to ye?" My voice was hollow. *Lord, help us, please. Help him.*

"Hurry, Tormod," Seamus said. "He's deadweight an' not walking out o' here on his own."

Seamus beneath one arm, and I the other, we dragged him, his head lolling forward in a faint.

Slowly we made our way back through the corridor and out of the doorway. The weight of his body was tremendous and the blood from his wounds slippery in my hands. The heavy, copper smell of it filled the dark space. His agony seemed to echo against the walls of my mind.

We came at last on the foul pit just as the carving began to flare.

"They're coming," I said breathlessly. "Hurry, Seamus."

We nearly dropped him in the struggle to get him through the grate. Seamus went first while I gripped the Templar's vestments, my arms aching with the strain. Then I pushed as Seamus pulled, dragging the Templar close against the wall to freedom. Waiting. Listening.

One. Two. Three. We counted the guard's steps overhead. *Four. Five. Six.* "Now," Seamus whispered, and we took off for the shelter of the darkened alleys. I thought there'd be an outcry, men at our back. There was nothing, but the trip was agonizing. The Templar remained unconscious, his tunic soaked clear through. My arms and back burned with the effort not to drop him.

"Get up," said Seamus, taking on the whole weight of the Templar's body.

I leapt into the wagon bed, and together we lifted the Templar and laid him in the straw. With a dark, filthy blanket that had seen much use, we covered him, hiding the white of his vestments.

"Get up in the seat and drive," Seamus ordered, handing me the dagger. "Take him through the front gate. Use the power on the guard if ye have to."

"Wait," I said. "What are ye going to do?"

"Do as I say and don't question it. It's vital that ye both go on an' finish as ye were destined. Follow the map."

I wavered. How could I leave him here?

"Go, before it's all for naught." He took the walking stick from the wagon and unsheathed the blade. "I'll keep them occupied an' run, as soon as I know ye're safe away." His face was white, pleading.

"No. I cannot leave ye," I said.

He looked at me one last time, and in his face I saw that the decision was out of my hands. "I'm sorry, Tormod. For everything." He slapped the horse's flank with the flat of the blade. "Heyah!" The animal took off faster than I had expected, and it was all I could do to rein him back in and direct us toward the gate at the sedate pace the healer I had replaced would have.

I dared not look back, but focused all my attention on the gate ahead and the aura of the guards pacing above. *They're o' no concern,* I whispered. *Let the wagon through.* My head pounded this time with the effort.

The gate dropped, and I crossed the drawbridge. On the far side I pushed again, even though my stomach now was heaving from the mental effort I'd expended already.

North. I urged the horse along the road and away.

✠

Tuo da Gloriam.

The shout came at me across the distance of space and mind.

The clash of swords. Darkness. A yearning for death. Troubled eyes.

"No!" I snapped from the vision sense. "It was no' supposed to be this way! Ye said ye would leave. Ye said ye would escape."

Another life. Another cruel end. It was too much. This all was too much. I shook as if palsied, the tears rolling down my cheeks as I slumped over in the seat.

Hush ye now, Tormod. The Templar's soft Highland lilt whispered in my mind.

I sat up quickly and leapt into the back of the wagon beside him. "Seamus . . ." I whispered.

Let no' his sacrifice be in vain. His mind voice was full of grief. *We have yet a duty to fulfill.*

DESTINATION

I held a water skin to the Templar's lips, urging, willing him to drink. He did, but sparsely. It was almost more energy than he could expend. There was nowhere on the Templar's back that was not cut and welted.

"I can heal ye. Let me try," I pleaded.

"Ye've done too much already, Tormod. The power changes us, takes a toll every time it is used. Ye healed Seamus."

My head was pounding and my body felt drained. I hadn't realized why. "How did ye know?"

"I felt ye. It matters no'. We must leave here. The soldiers will be seeking us."

I didn't push the discussion. He was sorely injured. I got down from the wagon and watered the horse. How had this come to pass? I could not seem to make my mind work it through. The carving sat at my middle in the depths of my sporran, thankfully cool once again. I watched the Templar, sick with worry. Each time he shifted, the blood seemed to seep once more.

"Let's go." I let the horse have one last go at the water, then took it away and dumped the little left. "Do we still have the map?" he asked.

"Aye. They never took the saddlebags from yer mount." As he reached for it, he grimaced and his skin paled. "North and west from here."

We set out straightaway. In the quiet drone of the horse's tread, I thought about Seamus. Part of me wanted to talk to the Templar about what had happened, but another part of me was a coward whose throat filled with lumps and eyes filled with tears each time I tried to speak. It mattered not; the Templar had fallen into a pained sleep. I would not wake him. He needed rest and healing. I had to wonder if all that we'd been through, all that had happened, would be worth it in the end.

We traveled the low rolling hills for most of the day. Even in sleep, he winced each time the wagon jarred him. Exhaustion and pain issued from his body, and the feel of it twisted my insides. He woke several times, and at each interval I urged water on him.

By nightfall we were deep into a forest that marked the gradual ascent into a group of low-lying hills. The dark of the sky was a silken purple, the dots of the stars like fireflies above us. I decided to stop for a rest and drew up before a rippling basin of water, fed by a cascading fall over the jagged rock of the hillside. Cool mist surrounded the place.

Labored breath rang in my ears. I looked around disoriented. Steep rocks filled the space before my eyes. Feet stumbling. Climbing.

The carving in my sporran was burning. *Focus. Ground. Shield.*

"Templar Alexander . . ." I whispered. Fumbling, I drew the carving from the pouch as he woke and inched his way to the edge of the wagon bed.

He was pale and drawn, barely managing to sit as he followed the direction of my gaze. With a gasp that disappeared beneath the crash of the water, he crossed himself with reverence.

In the spray of the crystalline waterfall, a brilliant splayed cross was illuminated.

"What does it mean?" I whispered in awe.

"Look!"

I turned to find his gaze not ahead, but above. There in the sky directly atop us was the glow of the constellation that matched the one we had been staring at from the beginning. The constellation that marked the map.

"Behind the falls," I said. "An old man came this way."

With a torch made of a dried tree limb and a strip of my tunic, I led the way carrying the last of our supplies, his sword, and my dagger. The Templar had all he could handle lifting himself in his weakened state.

The climb was slow. In the dark, footing was unsure. The cool mist coated my skin, but I was warm beneath the carving's steady glow.

At the mouth of the cave I helped the Templar over the last of the climb. We stood on the ledge as he gathered strength, staring into the depths of the blackness. The crash of the water echoed with the beat of the land, and I listened, taking it deep inside me, then letting it drift out again.

The Templar stood beside me, suddenly stronger and steadier than he had been only moments before.

" 'Tis an ancient healing site," he said. "Can ye feel the power?"

"Aye," I said. "What is it?"

" 'Tis said that throughout our world there are places where the earth's power is concentrated, where the pulse beats strongest, and the heart of the land lives. This is one of them."

He took the torch and moved into the cave, shining the light on the walls. Images were scribed there, ancient and beautiful — older even than the ones on the astrolabe. I moved close, running my fingers along the nearest. There were symbols and pictures, and in the midst of it I saw a cross similar to that of the Templar Order. I saw things that were half man, half animal. And lines that ran in patterns with no beginning or end. "Can ye read it?" I asked.

"No. Perhaps if I had more time."

In the back of the cave we found the remnant of a long-dead fire. Twigs and old logs lay nearby. I stacked them and lit the bundle with the torch.

"Ye will need as many torches as we can make," he said. "The tunnels are black as pitch."

"I?"

He didn't speak for a moment. Then quietly he said, "They are coming, Tormod." He sat down beside the fire, staring into the orange glow of the flames. "We've spoken before o' the pebble dropped into the stream, aye?"

"Aye," I replied, remembering. "Ye said what we saw as the future could be changed."

"What I have seen has already begun to change, Tormod. Ye have changed it. This is yer legacy. Yer duty to fulfill." He reached for his sword, though the movement clearly sent pain cascading through him. He bared the blade from its sheath. "It is my duty to make sure ye have the chance."

"No," I protested. "This is no' a thing I can do alone. Ye cannot stay here." It was always all right when he was by my side, but I knew what he proposed.

"I must keep them from reaching ye. I have seen what is to come. It is vital that I protect ye. 'Tis my calling, though for a while I was no' very good a' it." He slowly began his exercises. "I don't have the endurance to travel the tunnels that lead off from here. There is no telling how far they twist beneath the mountain."

I had come far in overcoming my fear of the darkness, but this was different altogether.

"There is wood enough for several torches." He pointed his sword toward a pile of sticks in the corner. "Use the blanket. Make strips an' tie them to the top." He continued to work his body, readying for confrontation. His back was oozing fresh blood with movements that had to be painful, but he kept at it.

"How are ye feeling?" I asked.

He didn't answer immediately. "Tormod, our goal is within reach." His voice was strong and determined. "I will guard yer back an' do what I must."

I looked at the torch in my hand and dropped my head. "I am afraid," I said.

"Wise men fear, Tormod, but they don't let the fear stop them from accomplishing what they must."

"I am not worthy," I said. "I'm not like ye. I question His will. I'm no' good enough to be a Templar."

He looked up at me, compassion in his eyes. "O' course ye are, lad. A Templar is just one who believes, one who is called. Ye, Tormod, have been called. Do ye disbelieve that for a second?"

I thought on it. I felt the carving warm, now back inside my sporran, and remembered the many visions that had come to me over the past few months. "I know that I have been called. I just worry that when it comes time to do something about it, I will fail."

"We can only do our best, Tormod. 'Tis all that is asked o' us." It was so simple to him. His faith was stronger than any man I'd ever met.

"Are ye ready?" he asked, sheathing the blade.

I had enough food and water for several days. And as I lit the first torch from the embers of the fire, he approached.

I took a deep breath. "Aye," I said. "I am."

He nodded. "Pay heed to yer torch. If the light goes out it might mean the difference between life an' death. But if ye should lose it, look to yer other senses."

I gathered my things and he helped me bundle the rest of the torches into my plaid. I was ready, and yet so unready I wanted to beg him to come with me.

"Godspeed, lad." Something in his tone struck a strange chord in me.

"Ye will wait for me? Will ye not?" I asked, suddenly uneasy.

"Aye. As 'tis within my power to do so."

I should have been assured, but for some reason a dark shadow hung heavy between us.

"All will be as it should, Tormod. It will be as it must." He read my thoughts, just as he had always done, and that in and of itself was reassuring. I nodded and turned away. Holding the flaming torch before me, I began my journey into the belly of the mountain.

THE TUNNELS

The dark in the caves was different than any place I could ever remember. It surrounded me, pressing against the light of the torch. I could see no farther than the glowing gold of the flame. My first few steps were halting, as if there was no earth beyond the step I took; but as the sameness continued, I became, if not comfortable, less wary.

The smell of ripe earth and wetness in the air made my clothes damp on my body. The path I chose branched away from the main, yet I knew the way deep in my bones. An odd tug in my gut drove me forward.

Time passed with no way of accounting for it, save the burn of the torches and the curl of hunger in my stomach. I walked long, taking breaks when my legs were too tired to continue. I ate when I needed, slept when compelled, and woke when my body decided it was time.

The Templar was right. He would not have been able to make this journey. Though I was certain the carving was leading me along the correct path, I had no idea how far I had yet to go. I was down to one torch to which I tied strips of my tunic, but I knew there was coming a time when I would have nothing left to keep the torch alive. The thought made me extend my distance a little more each time I felt I could go no farther.

I pushed myself hard, making my way to the elusive place my body and the carving seemed to hunt. But during a rest I could delay no more, the flame that had become my only companion flickered and died.

When I awoke, it was to a blackness that was absolute. I cried out, feeling for my bundles and the staff that I had last used as a torch. Its end was warm, but there was no flame or ember. My light had gone. I could see nothing, not the walls of the cave around me, nor the tips of my fingers, though they were right before my eyes.

My heart beat so loud I could hear it in my ears, and my breath became short — as if along with the light, the air had suddenly disappeared.

It was then that I felt it, a sudden spark of warmth on my stomach, a heat so strong it was nearly pain. I scrambled to my knees and dug in my sporran. The glow of the carving was brilliant. It lit the space better than the best of my torches and gave off a path of sparkling light I knew to follow.

Moments later I stumbled into the cavern, barely able to believe my eyes; only in Heaven could there be such brilliance as this. The walls were lit from within.

In the center of the room an enormous pillar stood, one great stalagmite that seemed carved of ice. In a daze I moved toward it, holding the carving stretched out before me, prayer spilling from my lips. In the side of the pillar was a natural depression, a shelf that held something I knew eyes had not seen in over a thousand years.

To say that it was a bowl would be as like to describe the waterfall outside as a bit of rainfall. I placed the carving down on the ledge and, with a trembling hand, lifted the most fragile, beautiful vessel I had ever encountered.

Its brilliant white wood was hollowed and smoothed by loving hands. On the outer surface an intricate pattern of vines and roots wound in a delicate never-ending tracery. Tiny leaves covered bits and pieces, but never did they conceal or cut off the wonder of the curved vine.

While I held it, tingling warmth raced through me. Suddenly I knew what I was supposed to do. Slowly I placed the vessel into the upraised hands of the carving, and for a moment that lasted a lifetime I cradled them both.

CHOICE

From the tips of my fingers to the ends of my hair, energy crackled, whipping through my body like the wind.

Colors flared and swirled, taking my breath away. Beautiful. Vibrant. Life thrummed in and around me, and I was a part. Past, present, future — images flitted through my mind in a blur. Faces. Places. Births. Deaths. Generations of lives became my own.

They were protectors, linked in the duty this sacred vessel called me to fulfill. All were gifted, honest, dedicated, and strong. They were everything I longed to be, but knew I was not.

What was I doing? I was not brave nor strong. Everything I did was wrong. I would make a mistake, lose it or break it or give it to the wrong person. I was suddenly afraid. The responsibility was too much.

I willed my fingers to open, to break the hold the vessel had on me. As if in response, an image unfolded before me. A sword slack at the Templar's side. His eyes blank, caught in the vision state. A shadow on the wall grew large. A sword arced, a life-stealing blow.

No! It could not be. I had to go to him. He had to be warned. But how?

Focus. Details of the vision of the Templar came instantly at my call, clear and sharp. The sound of men moving up the rocks played in my ears, and the spicy smell of the herbs Ahram and his men used to clean their bodies filled my nose. I could not determine if the vision was of the present or future. Had it happened already or would it soon come to pass? All I wanted was to drop the vessel and rush to him, but I could not let go.

Ground. Gritting my teeth, I concentrated, seeking the still and silent place within the swirl of color. I locked mind and body into the depths of the earth. The power flowed through me from the ground at my feet, branching like a tree reaching for the heavens as the earth's magic filled my veins. Strong. Powerful. Potent. "What do Ye want of me?" I shouted.

And then it came to me. Choose. Accept or deny the duty set before me.

Shield. With a nearly effortless flick, I sent the well of power out toward the edges of my skin and looked down at the precious burden in my hands. Doubt fled. I needed the power of the vessel if I had any hope of saving him.

"I accept."

Two simple words brought the chaos to an end as my fingers slowly unfurled and the bowl and carving tumbled to the cave floor.

✠

I woke to blackness, but there was no fear of the dark within me. With a start I realized that the holy vessel was not in my hands. Scrambling, I reached for the carving and tucked it in my sporran. Then I gently wrapped the bowl in my plaid.

With a sense of purpose and direction I left the cavern. The cool scent of damp earth hung in the air and a new awareness of the land's power filled me.

I ran, as I had when this whole trek began. The thud of my feet echoed in the tunnels and time passed in a blur. Fear for the Templar and terror that I would be too late pushed me nearly beyond my limits.

But then, from a distance I felt him. *Alexander!* I reached — joy and relief so heady I could barely breathe — and saw the vision that held him.

Me. I saw myself running through the dark of the tunnels. Now.

Tormod! Go back!

CONFRONTATION

I stumbled, feeling the lash of his anger. *Take it an' go. Damn ye, lad!*

But it was too late. I burst into the cave from a tunnel tucked in a fold of rock at his right, just as Philippe's soldiers rushed from beneath the falls. The Templar was as I'd seen him in the vision, his sword slack by his side, his eyes glazed, as battle cries bounced off the walls around us. I screamed and dove in front of him, my hand sweeping down and ripping the sword from his lax fingers.

It was heavy but felt right in my palm. I brought it up just as the first man came at me. The crack of his blade on mine brought me alive and I attacked with a vengeance, determined to protect the Templar until he could recover.

Ahram appeared at my side. Bakir and Fakih were at the cave's entrance heavily engaged. The Templar was suddenly behind me, out of his daze and shouting for his sword. I turned, distracted, and made to toss it to him just as the blade of the man before me snaked past my guard.

"No!" I screamed, filled with the knowledge of what would happen. As if time tried to reverse itself, the world slowed. Ahram dove toward us, his scimitar arcing down just as the sword of our attacker met its mark.

Blood from the man's arm splashed the runes on Ahram's face. I whirled and watched the Templar fall to his knees, clutching the blade in his chest.

"No! This will not be!" I drew the carving from my sporran, tossing off the plaid that covered the bowl. As the two reunited in my hands, the power of the land flared to life once more. Heat and color burst within me. Anger flooded my mind.

Men stopped midbattle, stumbling back, screaming in terror as a hot wind tore a circle around my body. I felt their fear and wanted them to suffer. I could think of nothing but destruction.

The blood in their bodies began to surge. I felt hearts pumping harder and faster and focused the power, unmoved by their screams.

Stop, Tormod! The Templar's weak command broke into my haze. *We are no' meant to use the power this way. Ye're a Templar. Ye're o' the light. Push it away.*

I was lost, confused. Staring around, I saw men cowering, white, bleeding. Others, released from my hold were clambering out of the cave.

"What have I done? Lord, what have I done?"

I turned to the Templar, begging for guidance,

dropping to his side. He was fading. Moving beyond. Leaving me.

"Please, Lord," I begged. "I'll do anything Ye ask, be anything Ye need. Please help me, just this once!"

Power rose again at my call, illuminating the cave with the brilliance of day. Heat suffused me and, as I had done before, I used the shield command to push it out to the edges of my skin. With the vessel still tight in my fingers, I laid it on his chest and focused on the wound.

No. His command was absolute. *The effort will steal yer strength. Take it from here, Tormod. This time ye will do as I say. Ye will change the outcome. I have seen it.*

And then, the Templar was no longer in my mind. He was closed off to me. Slowly I watched his body grow still.

"Ahhh!" My cry was that of a bairn torn from the arms of its mother. "No, Lord." I sobbed.

Ahram was beside me. "Tormod. More are coming. I'll see to him. There's nothing more you can do."

I could barely hear him through my grief. And then his hands were on me, heavy. Sharply, he dragged me to my feet. "Go, boy! He gave his life for you. Be gone from here, now!"

I stood, wavering, barely comprehending Ahram's dark eyes, snapping with anger. "Get out and run!"

Understanding came on me in a rush. I grabbed my plaid and threw it over the carving and bowl. I could feel the life pulse of men beyond the falls and bolted into the nearest corridor as darkness embraced me and I ran for my life.

AFTERMATH

Night was as day. I could sense nothing of the turning of time in the corridors beneath the mountain. And yet I moved through the blackness with ease. Tears streaked my cheeks, and the pain in my heart felt like a wound. He was gone.

His face hung in the dark of my mind, white and still. I would never see him again, never be his apprentice. The thought was a knife to my soul. I wanted nothing but to go back in time and erase what had happened, to die in his stead, or to stop running and lie on the floor of the cave and never rise again.

But even in this black hour, I would not. I had accepted the charge given me. The holy vessel and its power were mine to safeguard. I had seen what it could do, felt the awesome temptation to use it for evil, and understood how dangerous it was unguarded in the world.

I did not believe myself worthy, but I would do my best to ensure that not only the Templar's sacrifice, but that of Seamus and all of the others who had died in its service, were not in vain.

The beat of the land echoed in the wash of my blood. With a burdened heart I made my way through the dark, out into the light of a new day.

THE END

AUTHOR'S NOTE

The main characters in this novel are fictitious, and their resemblance to persons living or dead is purely coincidental. I did, however, bend facts with some of the historical characters, placing them in situations and geographical locations that helped the plot, and, in the case of Hughes de Payens, endowed him with the vision sense. Montségur was not a base for the Knights Hospitaller, but a twist of history I used to introduce readers to another important military body of the time, and also to explain the advanced system of checks and balances the Templars established. Please forgive my suggestion that the Popes Boniface and Benedict were part of a secret upper-echelon sect of the Templar Order. Although there is no evidence of this, imagining it adds depth to the mystery and makes a better story.

There was a group of warrior monks, the Poor Knights of the Temple of Solomon (or Knights Templar), who were an important and influential political and military body that functioned for nearly two centuries in the Holy Land and on three continents. Sworn to vows of poverty and chastity, they were nonetheless one of the wealthiest and most powerful governing bodies during the Middle Ages, with an impressive maritime presence. Their work in banking and finance was the precursor of many of the financial systems in use today. At their height they were the protectors of the treasuries and crown jewels of both France and England.

I came across the history of the Templars accidentally, while researching Scotland for an adult novel I was doing at the time. I was immediately drawn into their intrigue, and the more research I did, the more I felt the need to write about them. Their story demanded that I find and develop a knight of character and caring. Little did I know that I would find two.

ACKNOWLEDGMENTS

To my boys, Jim, James, and Conor: Your influence is clear on every page. You have my thanks and love, always.

To my fabulous editors Andrea Davis Pinkney and Eleni Beja: I can't thank you enough for taking a chance on a newcomer and embracing this completely insanely complicated little novel.

Special thanks are also given to Walter Lorraine, David Macaulay, Allen Say, and Fran Hodgkins, friends who each in their way, spearheaded this project into being. To Em S.K. Michael S. Kaulback, Grand Commander of Knights Templar of Massachusetts and Rhode Island, my Templar historian, for checking and rechecking all of the facts pertaining to the Templars, you have my undying gratitude. To Karen Brooks, for querying and calling me on the many details of fourteenth-century life. To Wolfman, for catching the porcupine and reminding me about the myths surrounding werewolves in the dark and superstitious time. And, finally, an enormous thank you to my favorite women: Eden Edwards, editorial coach extraordinaire, and Mary Plourde and Kim Biggs, whose constant and amazing insight into the detail of characters and place I could not have done without. To my mom and Ralph, thank you for always being there; I love you both. To my niece Amanda: You will love book two. It's all you, babe.

To Michael Baigent, Richard Leigh, and Henry Lincoln, the authors of *Holy Blood, Holy Grail*, I give my unending thanks, for so many of the backstory details that launched my love of research and of the Templar intrigue.